MYSTERY AT RUSTLERS' FORT

by Troy Nesbit

illustrated by

John Walter

WHITMAN PUBLISHING COMPANY • Racine, Wisconsin

CONTENTS

1   **A STRANGE QUARREL**

A heavily loaded station wagon, with a small, two-wheeled baggage trailer hitched behind, stood in front of Park headquarters on the North Rim of the Grand Canyon.

"Let me look," Phil McKenney said, bending over the big map that his cousin Buzz Fletcher had spread out on the front fender. "Where's our camp going to be?"

Buzz pointed. "See—that's the edge of the Grand Canyon. This pencil mark shows where we are going to camp. We're going to be near the edge of a side canyon."

"I want to see, too. Can I get out and look, Mommy?" This question came from Buzz's eleven-year-old sister Kitsy who sat in the front of the station wagon with her mother.

"Better not," Buzz said with a grin. "The Chief told me he'll be ready to start any minute, and you know how he is."

The Chief was Herbert Fletcher, Phil's uncle and Buzz's

father. Everybody called him "Chief"—his friends, his students at Red Rock College, even his children. He had earned the nickname because every summer he headed a scientific expedition into some remote place to find out about wild animals and their habits. This year his work promised to be especially exciting. The Chief was going to look for mountain lions on the North Rim of the Grand Canyon. And for the first time Phil had been allowed to come along.

"You boys better get in now," said the smiling, round-faced woman in the front seat.

"Okay, Aunt Amy." Phil quickly took his place in the second seat of the station wagon which was crammed full of baggage and scientific equipment.

More slowly, Buzz folded the map and eased his tall, lanky frame into the space beside Phil.

A moment later the Chief bustled out of Park headquarters where he had been talking to Boyd Blake, the Ranger Naturalist.

"Did Buzz tell you the news?" he asked. "We've got a much better campground than I'd hoped for."

"How do you know it's better if you haven't seen it?" Kitsy asked.

The Chief grinned. He was used to Kitsy's blunt ways. As he drove along the blacktop highway, he explained. He had expected to stay in some wild spot where they would really rough it. Instead, they would be living in relative luxury, with a ready-made fireplace and camp table. There was even a faucet where spring water had been piped right into the center of the campsite. The reason for their good luck was that the Park Service had started to build a big public campground on the spot. Then they had run out of money, after only one fireplace had been completed. It was in a wild area where tourists had never camped before.

"How do you know somebody isn't there already?" Kitsy demanded.

"Somebody is," the Chief answered. "We're going to kick him out."

At this his wife looked a little troubled. "Herbert, do we *have* to do that?"

"Don't worry. Boyd Blake says the man who pitched his tent there yesterday will want to leave, but he doesn't know it yet. I have a message for him that seems to be a call for him to go home in a hurry. Blake says that Headquarters got a telephone call this morning from the fellow's town, and he has to go right back where he came from."

Phil smiled to himself. Anybody who could wangle the Chief into running errands had to be pretty smart. The Chief was the kind who *sent* people on errands.

"What happened?" Aunt Amy asked with a touch of concern in her voice. "Did somebody die—or what?"

"I don't know," her husband replied. "It was none of my business, and Blake and I were both in a hurry, so I didn't ask. It must be bad news of some kind."

What a guy! Phil thought to himself. The Chief was so single-minded about his work that he didn't even ask an obvious question. At the same time, the Chief did get things done. That was what made him a fine scientist.

They went on in silence for a while, winding through open parks that lay between forested hills. Then the Chief slowed down, pushed back the Stetson hat from his forehead, and leaned intently over the steering wheel, watching the right side of the road with great care.

"Keep your eyes open, kids," he ordered. "The turnoff we want isn't marked—it's just a fire road."

Phil nudged Buzz and asked, "What's a fire road?"

"Just a track cut out of the woods so men can get in if they have to fight a forest fire. Hey, Pop!" Buzz yelled suddenly. "Looks like you just passed a turnoff."

Sure enough, there was a dim road. The Chief stopped and backed up, then shifted into low gear. The station wagon and trailer started down the steep, winding dirt road that had been deeply rutted by rains. Less than half a mile from the blacktop, they came to the bottom of the hill, and before them lay one of the beautiful natural meadows that nestled in among the heavily wooded surrounding areas. Aspens mingled with fir trees on the slopes that enclosed the meadow on all sides. The spot seemed a million miles from anywhere—except for one thing. On one side, near a fir tree and a couple of big aspens, stood a Chevrolet sedan and a khaki-colored tent.

"Is this the place?" Buzz asked.

"It must be," his father replied. "We'll see if anybody's home. Maybe the man's gone fishing. That's what Blake thought he was going to do."

"Where could anybody catch fish around here?" Phil asked in perplexity. He hadn't seen a single stream or lake since they came up into the vast wooded National Park area.

"There's wonderful trout-fishing down in a few of the side canyons," the Chief answered. "Big creeks gush right out of the canyon walls in some places. But up here on what they call the Kaibab Plateau, there are just a few springs and little ponds."

The station wagon pulled slowly ahead through the soft grass, and as it neared the campsite a big man stepped out of the tent. A small woman appeared from the far side of the Chevrolet.

"Beautiful spot you've got here," the Chief commented. "Are you Mr. Post?"

The big man looked surprised and said, "As a matter of fact, I am. But how did you know?"

"The Rangers told me you were here and they sent this message for you." The Chief handed over an envelope.

"Can we get out?" Kitsy whispered to her mother.

"I guess so, but don't get in these people's way," her mother answered a little uncertainly.

Mr. Post scratched his bald head, and his face flushed as he read the letter over a second time.

"What is it, Monte?" his drab little wife asked.

"Here, read it yourself," he said irritably and started for the tent, ignoring his visitors. Then suddenly he turned and shouted, "You can't have this camp. I got here first."

"But, Monte, we'll have to leave!" his wife exclaimed.

Phil, who had gone with Buzz to the nearby faucet to

get a drink, watched the tense scene and wondered what in the world could be going on.

"Look, Mr. Post," the Chief said quietly, "we don't want to drive you away. The Ranger simply told us he was sure you'd be leaving when you got the letter. I'm sorry if it's bad news. Is there anything we can do to help?"

"Nothing but go away," Mr. Post answered angrily.

"But, Monte, we have to leave," his wife persisted. "There's no reason why these people can't stay."

"Shut up. You keep out of this, Margaret. You'll stay right here and I'll be back in a few days."

"I wouldn't dream of staying here. I'd be scared to death," the little woman wailed.

Mr. Post seemed to pull himself together. "Be sensible, Margaret. This is our vacation. Nothing will happen to you here. I'm sure I can come right back. The police will get it straightened out in no time."

"I don't care. I couldn't possibly stay here alone."

"Mr. Post," the Chief broke in, "I hate to seem to take advantage of some misfortune of yours, but let me explain. I am engaged in scientific work, and the Park Service people feel that this is the place where I should have my head-quarters. It's the center of a wild area that next year will be filled up with tourists. For instance, the Ranger Naturalist tells me that a mountain lion has his haunts very close to this spot—"

"You see, Monte!" Mrs. Post's voice squeaked with fear. "I wouldn't dream of staying here alone. Lions!"

"I hope you understand my position," the Chief went on. "I'm not just a tourist. If I were, I could stay any place and enjoy myself and not bother you. But I must set up a permanent camp, with all my equipment, for the summer."

"Oh, dry up! Let me think!" Mr. Post exclaimed, and he stomped over toward his car.

Without another word, his wife started picking up the freshly washed breakfast dishes and stowing them in a cardboard carton.

"Is there anything we can do?" Aunt Amy asked, getting out of the station wagon.

"Oh, thank you. Yes, I guess you *could* help. Mr. Post is so upset. Perhaps your boys would take the tent down. We really do have to hurry," Mrs. Post murmured.

Aunt Amy beckoned to Phil and Buzz. "Mrs. Post says she'll be grateful if you'll take the tent down and roll it up," she said quietly. "Herbert, you and I are just in the way here. Let's walk up the road."

Phil wasn't exactly sure where to begin on the tent. Camping was new to him. But Buzz was an old hand. He motioned for Kitsy to come and help. By now Mr. Post was striding off across the meadow, as if he had to move around rapidly to clear his thoughts.

The tent was a simple, rectangular affair with a ridge pole and side walls that came up straight about three feet. It was pegged down all around, and inside it two neatly made-up cots stood on the dirt floor. Quickly, Buzz and Phil carried the cots outside. Then, while Kitsy and Phil held the upright poles, Buzz pulled the stakes out of the ground. A minute later, Buzz relieved Kitsy and the two boys lowered the tent to the ground.

"You're learning, Phil," Buzz said cordially. "Now we just take the poles out, fold the canvas, and the job's done."

They had the tent almost rolled up when a bellow sounded from across the meadow. Mr. Post came running toward them.

"What do you numbskulls think you're doing? Get away from there! You can't drive me out of this camp!"

"Monte, please! I asked them to help. We *have* to go. I know you hate to have your vacation spoiled but—" Mrs. Post's voice trailed off.

For a moment the big man looked as if he intended to hit somebody in his fury. Then he slowly relaxed.

"All right, I'll go." He turned toward the Chief and Aunt Amy who had returned to the station wagon. "But I'm warning you—I'm coming back in a couple of days. *I am going to have this campground.* I'd advise you to leave now and save yourselves trouble."

"Mr. Post," the Chief said with an angry tone coming into his voice, "don't threaten me. If you have any complaints, make them to the Rangers."

"Baloney! I'm warning you—get out of here!"

The whole Fletcher party climbed into the station wagon, feeling very uncomfortable, and watched the man and his wife heave things into their car.

After a while a slow grin spread over Buzz's long, lean face. "Now I know how it feels to inherit a million dollars," he commented to Phil.

"What are you so happy about?" Phil asked. "I wish we were out of here. Don't you feel kind of mean, running these people away from their camp?"

"Take it easy. We didn't chase them off. The letter did. But just look at all the work we don't have to do. That's what I mean by inheriting a million. We can pitch our tent right where that fellow had his. The ground is smooth and level. It's ditched all around, so we don't have to dig."

"Ditched?" Phil asked. Although they were going to camp out for the rest of the summer, they had stayed in motels on the way down from Red Rock in Colorado. The Chief was in a hurry to "get into the field," as he said, and he had driven long hours every day. Consequently Phil had never seen the process of putting up a tent.

"Sure," Buzz said. "You always dig a trench all the way around a tent and bank earth up against the canvas. Otherwise, when it rains, water will run right under the edge and soak you. Remember, we'll be sleeping on the ground."

"I thought you said our tent has a canvas floor—"

"It does. But you'd be surprised how much water will come through it if you haven't dug a trench."

Phil looked with considerably more interest at the Posts' tent site. "I bet the Chief will cop that place first. Won't you, Chief?" Phil said jokingly.

"I wish I could," his uncle replied, "but it's not large enough for my wall tent. The joke's on you. Buzz and you will have to level off a great big place *and* ditch around it. Then, when you've finished doing that, you can put up your little umbrella tent on Mr. Post's site."

"Uh! There's always a catch," Buzz groaned.

Mr. Post was now working frantically, tossing stuff into his car. Before long he was ready to leave.

"Did you put in your fishing tackle box, dear?" Mrs. Post called out to him.

"It's in that mess somewhere," he shouted back. "You got all your stuff?"

She nodded.

"Let's go." He started the engine, and when he had turned his car around, he leaned from the window to call, "I'm warning you folks again. I'm coming back here in a few days to finish my vacation."

"Whew! What a guy!" Phil said.

"Herbert, do you think we *should* stay? He may come back and make it unpleasant for us," Aunt Amy said.

"Of course we'll stay," her husband answered. "We have to stay here because of that mountain lion's travelway Blake told me about."

"Travelway—what's that?" Phil wanted to know.

As the Posts' car roared away up the quiet little valley, the Chief answered, "It's a regular route a lion follows looking for food. As long as he gets something to eat along his route, he uses it over and over."

The Chief opened the door of the station wagon.

"You mean he has a beat, like a policeman?" Phil asked in astonishment.

The Chief nodded. "Come on, hop out."

"Policeman—that reminds me," Kitsy said as she slid out of the seat, "what do you suppose that grouchy old Post was talking about the police for?"

"For the love of pete! We have better things to think about," the Chief said briskly. "First off, we're going to stretch our legs before we do any work at all. I'll show you something you'll never forget."

Without unpacking a thing, the five of them left the station wagon and trailer near the fireplace, then swarmed across the meadow after the Chief. They were all glad for a chance to get some exercise after the long, hot days on the road. There was no trail, and they had to step over fallen logs when they reached the woods at the end of the meadow. The ground sloped gently downward. Then suddenly there was nothing but empty space ahead.

Phil stopped in amazement. "Something sure must have happened here!" he exclaimed. There was wonder in his voice, and curiosity, and even a little fear, as he looked outward and downward. Beyond and below him was the biggest hole he had ever seen—in fact, the biggest hole in the world.

"Happened is right!" Buzz exclaimed. "The Grand Canyon!"

"It's a mile deep and ten miles wide, and some of the rocks down there are several hundred million years old," the Chief said.

"How do *you* like it?" Buzz asked, looking down at Kitsy.

"It's—it's too big!" Kitsy answered in a very small voice, and she stepped back from the edge of the precipice.

They were all quiet for a while, just looking at the great pinnacles and chasms and the bands of different colors that showed in the rock. At last the Chief said, "I hate to spoil your fun, but we have a camp to set up."

Reluctantly they all turned away—even Kitsy who was fascinated while at the same time she felt scared.

On the way back to the campsite, Phil had a wonderful sense of joy. Here was a great, wild country into which he could expand. For the first time since he was in the eighth grade, he didn't have to spend the summer cooped up answering the telephone in his father's small real estate office. It had seemed to Mr. McKenney that he was teaching his son a useful occupation—"breaking him into the business," he said. But to Phil all the work in the office was utter boredom and just a plain waste of time.

Except for short trips with his high school basketball team or for tennis tournaments, Phil had never been away from home before. He had never camped out, as Buzz did every summer. For a long time Phil had wanted to see the wild places that Buzz and Kitsy talked about. The Fletchers had asked him to come with them this year, partly because he and Buzz were good friends and partly because two such husky boys could do a great deal of work that would help the scientific expedition. Aunt Amy, as well as the Chief, was a naturalist. Her specialty was birds, and she had a big project planned, so she wanted to be free from work around camp as much as possible. The boys knew they would be expected to lend a hand when she didn't have time for such chores as washing clothes and cooking.

Phil was aware that he lacked experience. Right now he felt as he sometimes did before a tennis tournament when he was going to meet an opponent against whom he'd never played. He was a little worried but he was determined to win. He had made up his mind that he would like the outdoor life and learn the skills that went with it.

"HE'S COMING BACK!"

Back at the campground the Chief was full of bustle and hustle. He handed out chores to everyone. First Buzz and Phil had to prepare a level space for the big tent which the Chief, Aunt Amy, and Kitsy were going to occupy. It was a wall tent—the same kind that Mr. Post had, but twice as large. In addition it had an awning, or fly, that extended out in front to give shade and protection from rain. Long aspen poles had to be cut to hold up the fly, and ropes had to be tied to nearby trees to moor it securely. Then, while Kitsy and her mother set up three cots and spread them with blankets, the boys went to work on their umbrella tent. This one, unlike the other, had a canvas floor and only one upright pole in the center, with metal supports sticking out from it like the ribs of an umbrella. On the floor, the boys rolled out their sleeping bags and stowed away their two small, sturdy suitcases.

Soon camp was beginning to take shape. The Chief had assembled an aluminum worktable and set it next to his tent, under the fly. Then with the help of Phil and Buzz he opened the trailer and took out cameras, a small file case, books, a tape recorder, a heavy storage battery, and other scientific equipment. These were placed at one end of the big tent.

"When do we eat?" Buzz demanded at last. It was long past noon.

"As soon as you set up the gasoline stove," his mother answered. "We won't bother with a campfire for lunch. Kitsy, open up these cans of chili."

As Kitsy walked over to the heavy wooden camp table, her eyes caught something on the ground. "Hey! Look what I found!" she yelled. "Mr. Post's letter." She ran and grabbed it before either Phil or Buzz could reach it.

"Hurry up—open it! What does it say?" Phil demanded.

"Oh, phooey! Empty!" Kitsy said in disgust. "It's only the envelope."

"I sure wish I knew why that guy had to leave," Buzz said.

"If he keeps his word, we'll find out when he comes back

and tries to chase us away from here," Phil remarked.

Just then Kitsy grabbed Phil's arm. "Look!" she whispered.

Phil turned. There, across the camp and beyond the water faucet which was just a naked pipe about four feet high, stood a deer. The animal seemed uninterested in their presence and nibbled at a piece of watermelon rind that the Posts had carelessly left on the ground.

"Look, folks! A deer—over there!" Phil whispered to the others. "Don't scare it!"

"*Odocoileus hemionus macrotis,*" the Chief said in a matter-of-fact tone of voice.

Phil looked at him in amazement. "What did you say?"

"Don't pay any attention to Herbert. He's just showing off," Aunt Amy laughed. "What he said was the scientific name for a mule deer. See her long ears? That's why she's called a mule deer. They often become very tame. Probably she got used to people when the men were building this campsite."

"Can I feed her, Mommy?" Kitsy asked eagerly.

"You can*not,*" her father answered.

"Why not?"

"It's not safe."

"But she hasn't any horns—she couldn't hurt us," Phil said.

"She's got hoofs," his uncle answered. "And she knows how to use them. You can go close to her, but don't feed her and don't pat her, either."

Though it didn't seem sensible, Phil supposed his uncle was right. After all, the Chief was a biologist. It was his job to know things like that.

"Here, you boys set the table," Aunt Amy said. "We're going to eat in a minute."

All during lunch, Phil kept an eye on the deer. She was a handsome reddish brown. Her small white tail which had a black tip at the end made a funny contrast to her large ears which stood up twitching, always on the alert. At the clatter of a fork on an aluminum plate, she would bound away a few yards with a stiff-legged kind of grace. Then slowly the gentle-looking animal would work her way back, always getting closer and closer to the table.

"Now," the Chief said, swinging his small, wiry body away from the bench, "you kids wash up the dishes. After that, I want you to bring in a big pile of wood and kindling. Amy and I are going to the post office for mail. It should be distributed by now."

Kitsy washed, Buzz wiped, and Phil gathered up the empty tin cans and scraps. As he started for the big garbage can which stood to one side of the wall tent, he saw the deer approaching. He moved slowly, quietly toward her. She halted and stared with interest as he inched forward. Unable to resist the impulse, he held out a half-eaten slice of bread.

The doe took a step forward, sniffed at the bread, then greedily snatched it and ate it. There was no more food to offer her, so Phil just held out his hand. The doe sniffed at his fingers. The temptation was too great. Phil reached out and stroked the short, coarse hair on her neck.

With lightning speed, one slender forefoot curled upward and slapped at him. The little hoof with its two sharp points tore at his right thigh, ripping his jeans and leaving a nasty gash in his skin. Phil let out a yell of surprise and pain and jumped back clumsily, dropping the garbage. In a couple of bounds, the doe was a few yards away. There she stopped and began calmly to chew at something on the ground.

"Phil! What happened?" Kitsy cried. She and Buzz came running.

"The deer kicked me," Phil answered.

"Wow! Look at you! You're bleeding. Kitsy, get the first-aid kit," Buzz exclaimed.

While Kitsy rummaged in the trailer, Phil sat down on the bench at the camp table. "I sure was dumb," he complained. "I did just what the Chief told us not to do. I patted that deer."

"Here," Buzz said, taking the first-aid kit from his sister. "I'll fix you up. Kitsy, you ought to give that deer a good talking-to."

Through the hole in Phil's jeans, Buzz doused sulfa powder over the gash, then covered it with a gauze dressing. "Now go change your pants, so the folks won't notice anything," he ordered.

Meekly and gratefully, Phil obeyed. When he emerged from the umbrella tent, Kitsy asked, "Does it hurt much?"

"Not too much," Phil said honestly. "I guess I'll live. Look, Kitsy, do me a favor. Don't tell your mother and father what a dope I was."

"Of course not," Kitsy answered in her flat, earnest way. "What do you think I am, a tattletale?"

Phil felt even guiltier now because he couldn't do his share of the wood gathering. But he did manage to limp up the hillside and break off a lot of dead limbs from fallen trees. Buzz carried most of the wood back into camp, since Phil's leg hurt him worse going downhill than it did going up.

At last the three of them had what they thought was a magnificent woodpile, and they sat down in the folding camp chairs in the shade of the fly to rest.

"Boy, there's a lot of work to do around a camp," Phil said.

"You don't know the half of it," Buzz drawled. "We're just starting. Wait till the Chief gets a project going. You'll see what work is. And I used to have to do it all myself. I'm going to write your mother a letter and thank her for letting you come along this summer."

"*You?* Write a letter?" Kitsy put in. "You haven't written thank-you letters yet for Christmas."

"I'm waiting till just before next Christmas to do that," Buzz answered. "That will remind 'em."

Phil was looking through the open flaps of the tent at a pile of equipment which the Chief hadn't yet sorted out. There were wire cages of two different kinds that interested him. "What are those things for?" he asked.

"Well, the squarish ones are Mom's," Buzz explained. "She's going to catch birds in them. Then she'll put bands on their legs and let 'em loose again. The cage is fixed like a trap that doesn't hurt the birds. The bands are to identify them. Somebody may catch some of the birds later on, and the bands will tell how long they've lived and where they've been and so on. The Chief says you'd be surprised how much scientists don't yet know about birds."

"What about the round things?"

"Those are cages, too. They're for bats. I don't know what the Chief's going to do with bats when he catches them. We'll find out later. Oh, we'll find out!" Buzz sighed in mock weariness.

Phil knew that Buzz was always putting on an act about work, but he knew also that his cousin planned to be a scientist just as the Chief was. Phil had no idea what he himself wanted to be, as long as it wasn't something that kept him inside an office.

Suddenly a thought came to Phil. "Say, I didn't see any gun in all that stuff we took out of the trailer."

Buzz looked surprised. "Gun? What do we want a gun for?"

"Why, for the mountain lions. Aren't they dangerous?"

"I don't know. All I know is the Chief never has a gun. He doesn't like 'em," Buzz answered.

"If you understand animals you don't need guns," Kitsy said positively.

"Well, phooey on you!" Phil said. "I don't care if you do understand a lion. He can kill you if he jumps on you."

"He won't," Kitsy said.

Phil wasn't so sure. Come to think of it, he had assumed that the Chief was going to hunt lions this summer and probably bring them back stuffed for the museum at Red Rock College.

"Well, how *are* we going to hunt them then?" he asked.

"Oh, we'll just watch them and take pictures and stuff —I think," Buzz answered.

Phil was still doubtful. He didn't feel at all happy that he'd have no protection from a mountain lion, and he remembered that there might be one quite close to camp right now. A gun was a thing he understood. He was on his high school rifle team, and he was a crack shot. Somehow, he felt disappointed that he wouldn't have a chance to use the special skill he had which seemed to go with an expedition into the wilderness.

"Hey," Buzz broke the silence. "We better hold a meeting. Kitsy, you're chairman. The question before the house is: Shall we sit here, calm as cucumbers, looking as if we'd done everything we're supposed to do when the folks come back? Or should we listen for the engine and then start doing things like crazy as they drive down the hill?"

Kitsy giggled. "Who's going to motion something?"

"Madam Chairman," Phil said, "you don't motion something, you move it."

"Madam Chairman," Buzz said, leaning back ostentatiously in his camp chair, "I move we don't make a move."

"All in favor, stand up," Kitsy said impishly.

"That's a dirty trick," Buzz protested. "You're not democratic. Phil's got a bum leg and you know I'm comfortable the way I am."

"Oops!" Kitsy said. "Here they come."

Buzz staggered to his feet. With one hand on his back he hobbled toward the station wagon. "Oh, Chief!" he groaned. "You shouldn't have gone away. We nearly killed ourselves working."

The Chief looked at the woodpile and then back at the boys. "I know. I sure feel sorry for you fellows. But it's going to be hard to find wood in the dark tonight after that little bit of kindling has started the fire."

"Want to hear the news?" Aunt Amy broke in. "I found out why the Posts left in such a hurry. Boyd Blake told me that somebody broke into Mr. Post's jewelry store in the town of Kanab and robbed it over the weekend. The man who works for Mr. Post discovered the burglary this morning and phoned Park headquarters. He knew the Posts were spending their vacation here. Thousands of dollars' worth of things were taken from the safe. Isn't that something?"

"Whoo-eee! No wonder he went home!" Phil said.

"Well, he didn't need to be so mean to us," Kitsy remarked. "We didn't steal his old jewelry."

"I don't know—" Buzz said thoughtfully. "When you're sore about one thing, I guess you kind of get sore about everything else, too."

"Did they catch the robber?" Phil asked.

"I don't know," Aunt Amy answered. "I guess not, or there wouldn't have been so much excitement."

Phil thought a minute. He had learned a few things about business while working in his father's office. "Now I see why Mr. Post was so sure he'd be coming back here. If you have that much stuff in a store, you have insurance on it. He'll just collect the insurance, then turn up here again to finish his vacation."

"I *know* he's coming back," Kitsy added. "He said he was and he meant it."

3   PHIL'S SECRET DECISION

"Hey, Aunt Amy, where's that copy of the Denver *Post* you brought back day before yesterday when you went for mail?" Phil asked. "I want to look at the sports section."

His aunt stopped typing. She and the Chief were busy answering letters, and there had been a lull in activities for Phil and Buzz.

"It's on the box at the foot of my cot in the tent."

Phil brought out the fat Sunday newspaper and spread it on the camp table. There had been so much work to do that he hadn't had a minute to check baseball scores. As he turned the pages, Buzz looked over his shoulder.

"Wait a minute," Buzz said.

A page full of advertisements for camping equipment and gadgets of all kinds had turned up.

"Look at that—that's neat! A salt and pepper shaker

that works from both ends," Buzz said with a grin.

"Look at this." Phil pointed to a large ad with a coupon.

"Vermilion Cliffs!" Buzz exclaimed. "Say, we went right past that place on the way into the Park. It was just after we crossed the Colorado River on that big bridge. Remember those big red cliffs?"

"That's right," Phil said excitedly. "Say, there's a lot of red cliffs down in the canyon here, too. We saw them when we looked down over the edge. There must be uranium around this place, too."

"I bet there is. The Vermilion Cliffs aren't very far away from here. Wouldn't it be something to find uranium!"

"The Mighty Midget!" Phil said. "You know what?

I'm going to buy one. I've got the twenty dollars that my folks gave me for the summer. I'm sure going to buy one!"

"Buy what?" asked Kitsy.

"This Geiger counter," Phil replied.

"What's a Geiger counter?"

"Don't you know? It's a gadget that tells you where to find uranium ore. You just carry it along with you, and if it starts making a racket you know you've found a place to start digging a mine. You send your money to this place in Denver and they mail it to you. The man in the picture here found a mine and he's rich already."

"I don't want to be rich," Kitsy remarked. "Rich people don't camp out."

"What's going on over here?" asked the Chief, who had apparently finished his letter writing.

"I'm going to buy a Geiger counter and go prospecting for uranium," Phil explained.

"Nonsense," the Chief snorted. "Do you know how much those things cost?"

"They cost four ninety-five." Phil showed him the ad.

"Don't believe everything you read. A usable Geiger counter will cost at least ten times that much."

"Aw, Chief—" Phil began.

"And what's more," the Chief went on, "we're going to be so busy we won't have time for prospecting."

"But maybe we could make an important scientific discovery with a Geiger counter," Phil persisted, trying to think up arguments that would appeal to his uncle.

"Well, if we were geologists, which we aren't, and if we had a good instrument, which we can't get, we might make a discovery. But we're on a different kind of expedition. You don't look for mountain lions with a Geiger counter."

Phil found himself wondering why a naturalist couldn't be interested in rocks as well as animals. But he knew well enough that the main purpose of the Fletchers' expedition was to find out more about the lives of animals and birds.

"Aw, come on, Pop," Buzz put in. "If Phil wants to spend his allowance on a Geiger counter, I don't see why he can't. It's his money, isn't it?"

"I've already told you why," the Chief answered.

"But I don't see—" Phil began.

"If you don't see, you don't see. But this is the last I want to hear of the subject."

The Chief was obviously irritated. But Phil was irritated, too. He felt that his uncle was treating him like a little kid. He might have kept on arguing with his own father, but he was a guest of the Fletchers and he didn't want to start the summer by making his uncle sore now. Nevertheless it got Phil's dander up to have the Chief tell him what to do with his own allowance. The more Phil thought about it the more annoyed he grew. Suddenly he made up his mind. He was going to get a Geiger counter whether his uncle liked it or not.

As soon as the Chief went over to the station wagon, Phil tore the ad out of the paper and stuck it in his wallet. Buzz gave him a knowing look.

"What's that, Daddy?" Kitsy asked.

"What does it look like?" The Chief grinned as he pulled his head out of the rear end of the station wagon and dropped a big coil of something on the ground.

"A hose," Kitsy said. "Are we going to start a garden?"

"Hear ye! Hear ye!" her father announced. "You are all about to witness the installation of a modern, hygienic public health device."

"Mommy, what's he talking about?"

"Kitsy, your guess is as good as mine," her mother answered. "We'll have to wait and find out."

Without another word, the Chief screwed one end of the hose onto the faucet and then began stretching it out in the direction of the boys' tent. It went past the tent, to a clump of brush on the far side of an aspen tree.

"Come here, Buzz," the Chief said. "Poke the end of the hose up over that limb."

Thoroughly mystified, Buzz did as he was directed. Now the Chief fished some heavy cord out of his pocket. "Can you tie it in position so it won't slip?"

Buzz managed a kind of lashing around the tree limb.

"Now screw this on." The Chief handed him an ordinary garden hose nozzle. "Kitsy, turn the faucet on."

With her pigtails flying out behind, Kitsy ran to the faucet, and in a moment a strong spray of water poured out of the nozzle.

"All right, we're in business. Private shower bath."

"Herbert, where in the world did you get that hose?" Aunt Amy asked.

"Borrowed it off a fellow in the garage, while you were talking to Boyd Blake's wife."

What else would the Chief think up? Phil wondered. His uncle had kept them busy all day yesterday fixing things to make camp permanent and convenient. Phil had had some difficulty concealing the fact that his leg, which had been cut and bruised by the deer's hoof, was painful, but he had managed his share of the work without attracting attention to himself. A monstrous pile of wood had been assembled, although much of it remained to be chopped up. A big metal food-cupboard had been attached to a tree where it would be in the shade and out of reach of prowling animals. Then the boys had helped Aunt Amy set up a feeding station for birds at the lower end of the meadow. She wanted to attract as many birds as possible, so that she could watch them and take pictures. All this had been hot, sweaty work, and there would probably be plenty more of it. A shower, even if it was only ice-cold water, was sure a good idea.

Everybody except Kitsy was still admiring the Chief's invention, which gave a highly satisfactory spray behind its screen of bushes, when suddenly the water stopped running.

"Mommy," Kitsy called softly from her place by the faucet, "you better come see what that deer is doing."

Aunt Amy hurried toward the center of the campground. There stood the doe, peacefully chewing up a piece of paper.

Kitsy giggled. "She pulled your letter right out of the typewriter. Isn't she smart?"

"Oh, drat her! Now I have to do it over," Aunt Amy

fussed, shooing the animal away.

The deer bounded only as far as the boys' tent, then slowly walked on to the site of the new shower bath. Struck by a sudden inspiration, Phil stepped over to the faucet and quickly turned it on. There was an explosion of activity behind the bushes and the doe took off in great leaps across the meadow.

"That was mean!" Kitsy said indignantly. "Just because she kicked—" Then she caught herself before giving away Phil's secret about his encounter with the deer's hoof. Kitsy went on in a low tone of voice, "If you do anything like that again, Phil, I *will* tell on you!"

But Phil felt no sense of guilt whatsoever. He had partly evened up his score with that deer, and she was none the worse for it. There hadn't been much rain lately, and she probably needed a bath, anyway. She certainly hadn't been very scared, because she was approaching the camp again. Before she had come halfway, she stopped and looked intently in the direction of the road, twitching her ears. A moment later a Chevrolet appeared at the upper end of the meadow.

"I told you so," Kitsy said as the car drew near. "It's that mean old Mr. Post."

4

Monte Post was a totally different man today. "Howdy, folks!" he greeted them heartily. "How you making out?"

"Fine," Aunt Amy answered. "This is such a beautiful place!"

The Chief, looking a bit cautious, shook Mr. Post's hand and said, "Boyd Blake at headquarters told us about your bad luck."

"News sure does travel fast out here in the wilds," Mr. Post remarked with a grin.

"Do you know who robbed your store?" Kitsy asked.

Seriously, the big man answered, "No, the police haven't found out a thing yet, although they say they have some clues they're working on. Somebody cut the lock right out of the door and then pushed it open. Well, that's the way life goes. I expect things will turn out right in the end."

"Wouldn't you like a cup of coffee, Mr. Post?" Aunt Amy asked. "I was just going to fix some."

"I didn't come for that, but thank you, I don't mind if I do," he said genially.

"What *did* you come for?" Kitsy asked in her blunt way.

"Kitsy!" her mother protested.

Mr. Post gave a hearty laugh. "I had good reasons. Give me time and I'll tell you."

Phil watched as the big man heaved his legs over the bench that was attached to the camp table, took off his hat, and rubbed his bald head. It was hard to believe this was the same person who had put on such a scene the day of their arrival. Mr. Post seemed like a very good guy. Phil thought it might be fun to have him around, if indeed he had come back to finish his vacation.

"One reason I'm here," Mr. Post started in, "is to apologize to you good people. I guess I was kind of thrown by the news about the robbery, and I said a lot of things to you that I shouldn't have said. Can't remember exactly what I did say, but my wife tells me I wasn't a bit polite."

"Goodness! You don't need to apologize!" Aunt Amy exclaimed. "We felt badly about seeming to take advantage of your misfortune."

"That's nice of you to say so, ma'am, but I guess I was pretty cantankerous. I was sure upset."

Phil couldn't contain his curiosity about the burglary. "Did they get away with much stuff?" he asked.

"Yeah, plenty. About ten thousand dollars' worth, as near as I can figure." Mr. Post shook his head ruefully.

"I hope you had insurance on it!" the Chief exclaimed.

"Oh, sure. But it's one thing to have insurance and another to collect anything on it. Meanwhile, I'm losing business. You can't sell jewelry if you don't have any."

"I didn't realize Kanab was big enough to support a jewelry store," the Chief said.

"It's not very big, you're right. But there's a lot of money in the area. There's a uranium boom on, you know, and you'd be surprised how many prospectors are striking it rich—or at least selling claims for a lot of money. You wouldn't believe how many top-quality watches, for example, I can get rid of in a week."

"Do you sell Geiger counters?" Phil asked.

"No, that's not in my line. A couple of other fellows in town do, though. Are you interested in prospecting, young man?"

"I sure am!"

"Now, Phil," the Chief said a little sharply, "we've already settled that question."

"Did you ever go prospecting, Mr. Post?" Buzz asked.

"No, I've got too many other things to worry about. But for the moment I've decided to stop worrying about anything. I'm staying up at the big public campground, and I'm going to have a couple of days of fishing. I tried to persuade Mrs. Post to come along, but she's still too upset about the robbery."

Aunt Amy looked sympathetic and said, "I don't blame her."

"That leads me to the other reason why I dropped in on you folks," Mr. Post went on. "I suppose you found my fishing tackle box around here somewhere."

The Fletchers and Phil all shook their heads.

Then Kitsy said, "I heard you tell your wife you put it in your car."

"I certainly thought I did, but when I got home it wasn't there. Now I seem to remember that I left it behind my tent. I'll just go and have another look."

Phil and Buzz went with him and poked around in the brush at the back of the tent. But there was no box.

"What did it look like, Mr. Post?" Phil asked.

"Just an ordinary tackle box—green metal. It wasn't worth much, but I do fancy the flies I had in it. I tied most of them myself."

"Gee, somebody must have swiped it," Buzz said. "First they rob your store and then they steal your tackle!"

Mr. Post seemed to digest this remark. Then, with a look of concern on his face, he returned to the table to finish his coffee. "I don't want to alarm you good people," he said, "but somebody seems to have made off with my box. Is anything of yours missing?"

"Not a thing that we've noticed," Aunt Amy said.

Some of the bounce seemed to have gone out of him. "I guess this place is made for thieves. It's got a long record. Did the Rangers tell you kids about it?"

"About what?" Kitsy asked.

"About the horse thieves' trail and fort."

Kitsy shook her head, and Phil and Buzz crowded onto the bench across from Mr. Post, listening eagerly.

"Well, right across the ridge to the east is the beginning of one of the big side canyons that lead into the Grand Canyon. If you look hard enough over there, you can find a dim trail that goes down to the Colorado River. In the old days the trail passed through this meadow and up under that ledge you can see." He pointed to a small cliff that was visible above the tops of the trees.

"Well, what about the horse thieves?" Kitsy asked.

"They made the trail. They used to steal horses on the other side of the Grand Canyon, and they brought them across the river by a secret route. Then they drove them up Dry Bones Creek, across the ridge, and through this meadow. When they got here, they always stopped for a drink and a rest. This was the first place they could find water after they left the creek."

"You mean they put this water pipe in?" Phil asked.

Mr. Post laughed. "No, the plumbing is brand-new, but the water comes from a spring that the rustlers used. There's a kind of niche up there, underneath an overhanging ledge of rock. And there's a spring in the niche. The horse rustlers built themselves a kind of fort around it."

"No fooling!" Phil exclaimed. "Is the fort still there?"

"Sure. They built it good and solid in case they had to fight off the sheriff. It was a smart idea. They had the water *inside* the fort. And in this dry country, water is about the most important thing."

"How do you get up there? Can we go look?" Buzz asked eagerly.

"It's easy. See those two little aspens about fifty yards up the meadow? Well, right behind them you'll find a faint old trail. You follow it and you'll come out at the ledge where Rustlers' Fort is. If you keep going beyond the fort, you'll hit the blacktop road in no time. Fact is, the trail is a handy shortcut between here and the road."

"Mommy, can I go and look right now?" Kitsy asked.

Phil and Buzz glanced at each other. They wanted to go, too, but more than that they wanted to find out if this interesting character had any more stories to tell.

"There's plenty of time, Kitsy," said the Chief. "Wait till the boys are ready to go with you."

"Mr. Post," Phil asked, "when were those rustlers here?"

"Oh, before my time—maybe forty or fifty years ago, at least. But I'm doing all the talking. I understand you people are working on some sort of scientific stuff. What are you looking for?"

Phil groaned to himself. "Now we'll never get a chance to pump Mr. Post for more stories," he thought. "The Chief will start a lecture."

Phil was right. His uncle was more than happy to explain about the Fletcher expedition. When the Chief mentioned that he wanted to see Kaibab squirrels, among other things,

Mr. Post's face lit up. "Have you got a map? I can show you where you're sure to find some of those little fellows."

The Chief ducked into the tent to get his map case, and this gave Phil a chance he had been waiting for. "Mr. Post, do you know how much a good Geiger counter costs?" he asked.

"I've seen new ones price-marked anywhere from a hundred dollars up to a thousand," Mr. Post answered with a smile. "But I expect you might be able to pick up a secondhand one at quite a reduction. Prospectors are always going broke and selling things cheap."

At that moment the Chief returned with a huge topographical map of the area, and Phil tactfully dropped the subject of Geiger counters.

As Mr. Post marked a spot on the map, Phil asked, "Why do they call it Dry Bones Creek?"

"I don't know. Never heard," Mr. Post answered.

"I don't know either," the Chief remarked, "but I know how Bright Angel Creek got its name."

Mr. Post didn't seem much interested, but the Chief insisted on giving his explanation: "The first man who explored the Colorado River went down it in a boat in the 1870's. At one place he found a creek that was dirty and smelly, and he called it Dirty Devil Creek. Then, farther along, he saw a stream of clear fresh water pouring in from a side canyon. Naturally, he had to give that creek the opposite kind of name. So he called it Bright Angel."

Phil was reading other names on the map. At the point where Bright Angel Creek joined the Colorado River, he saw the words "Phantom Ranch."

"Is there really a ranch down there?" Phil asked.

Mr. Post brightened up. "There sure is, although I guess you'd call it a dude ranch. A lot of tourists go down into the Canyon on muleback, and they stay overnight at the Phantom Ranch. It's a real swanky joint, swimming pool and everything."

"Daddy!" Kitsy exclaimed. "Why didn't you tell us about that! Can we go?"

"As a matter of fact," the Chief replied, "I was saving it for a surprise. I was going to reward you kids—*if* you did a good job of work. We're going to make the trip down there in a couple of weeks."

"Mighty fine fishing in Bright Angel Creek," Mr. Post said. "But I guess I won't get any of it. I sure would like to catch the skunk that swiped my fishing tackle box. It seems to me that you good people ought to keep your valuable equipment locked up when you're away from camp."

"I don't think there's anything to worry about," the Chief answered. "Besides, one or the other of us will almost always be close to camp."

"Well, I'll be going," Mr. Post said. "I'll see if there are any trout flies worth buying at the store by the post office. If not, I'll just go on home. *Auf wiener schnitzel,* as the fellow said."

"We may drop in to see you sometime," the Chief said. "The store up here doesn't have much of any food, and Amy wants to go to the supermarket in Kanab."

"Let's make a date now, so I'll be sure to be there," Mr. Post said cordially.

"I haven't any idea which day we can make it," the Chief answered. "We'll just hope to find you in."

The minute Mr. Post was in his car, Phil said urgently to Buzz, "Come on, let's go to that old Rustlers' Fort."

The two long-legged boys started across the meadow at a fast clip, leaving Kitsy behind.

"Have you got any money?" Phil asked Buzz as they hurried along.

"A couple of dollars. Why?"

"Well, we may need it. When we go to Kanab, we're going to buy a secondhand Geiger counter with my twenty dollars, plus your two bucks."

Buzz thought this over. "Suppose we make a strike. If you put up twenty dollars and I only put up two, who owns the mine?"

Phil was silent until they located the beginning of the trail beyond the two aspen trees. He had been doing some mental arithmetic. "I'll lend you nine dollars, and that'll make us equal partners. But you'll have to pay it back out of the profits."

"What if we can't get a Geiger counter for twenty-two dollars?" Buzz asked doubtfully.

"Oh, sure we can. You heard Mr. Post say there are two stores in Kanab that sell them."

"Wait up!" Kitsy's voice came to them from down in the meadow.

The boys stopped.

"What a character that guy Post is!" Phil said. "When I saw him coming into camp, I was scared he was going to run us out of here with a shotgun. But he seems like a regular fellow."

"Yeah. I wish he'd come back. You wouldn't ever think

he was in the jewelry business, would you?" Buzz said.

"I don't know," Phil answered. "There are all kinds of people in all kinds of businesses. He probably makes a lot of money and doesn't have to work much, and that way he can go fishing all the time."

"Sure, you're absolutely right," Buzz said. "We can do the same thing when we get our uranium mine."

Kitsy caught up with them. All three clambered over some fallen rocks and found themselves on the ledge that Mr. Post had pointed out. Sure enough, there stood a little stone building that must have been the horse thieves' fort.

And beyond it at the other end of the ledge—

"Look!" Phil whispered to Buzz.

Disappearing through a grove of aspens on the steep slope was the back of a strange-looking man. He was shaped like a milk bottle with legs attached—small at the top and bigger and bigger all the way down. Another odd thing— although he was scrambling around on the hillside, he wore a business suit.

"Wonder what that bird was doing here," Phil said.

"Probably some tourist. The road isn't very far away, Mr. Post said. Let's look at the fort," Buzz answered.

Kitsy had opened the heavy door made of new planks.

The light from the doorway revealed a small, square room. Dimly outlined along one side they could see a new concrete trough into which water dripped from the native rock which made up the back wall of the fort.

As their eyes grew accustomed to the dimness, they realized that small streams of light came through half a dozen holes in the masonry, all at just about the eye-level of the two boys.

"By golly! Know what those are?" Phil said excitedly. "Those are loopholes where the rustlers could shoot their guns at anybody who was attacking them."

"This is neat!" Buzz exclaimed. "And say! Nobody could shoot through the door from the outside." There was a bulge in the gray rock of the ledge which did protect the doorway.

They went out and looked around. At their feet was the pipe that carried water from the spring, down the hill to the faucet.

"You can see our camp. Somebody could spy on us and we'd never know it." Phil paused. "Do you suppose that guy we saw a minute ago was spying on us?"

"Dopey," Kitsy said. "What would anybody want to spy on us for?"

5   THE DINOSAUR AND A MOUNTAIN LION

On the way down the hill, Phil began to limp. His sore leg was bothering him a little, although he hadn't noticed it coming up. Kitsy, lagging behind, suddenly called, "Hey, Buzz, don't go so fast. Can't you see Phil's leg hurts?"

Phil grinned appreciatively at the look of real concern on Kitsy's face. She was a good kid. She had kept loyally quiet about his run-in with the deer. The thought crossed his mind that he might ask *her* for some money, if the Geiger counter cost more than twenty-two dollars.

"Did you put a clean bandage on it today?" she asked Phil.

"Sure. It'll be well in a day or two."

They loafed on down the trail.

Suddenly Kitsy said, "Why do you suppose there's a new door in that old fort?"

"The Rangers must have put it there to keep animals and things from dirtying up our drinking water. Hey, did anybody shut it when we came out?"

"I did," Kitsy answered.

It sometimes annoyed Phil and Buzz that Kitsy, who was four years younger, was so much neater and more methodical than they could ever be. Still, her orderliness could be convenient. Right now it meant that they didn't have to climb back uphill and check on the door. Phil was perfectly sure that if she said she had closed it, she had done just that.

As the three of them stepped out of the trees into the meadow, they saw something that brought them all to a dead stop. An unfamiliar car was parked near the station wagon. And there, standing by the fireplace, talking to the Chief, was the bottle-shaped man they had seen sneaking off through the trees at the Rustlers' Fort.

"What's he doing here?" Buzz whispered.

"We better warn your folks we saw him spying on the camp," Phil said.

Buzz and Kitsy obviously shared Phil's slight feeling of alarm. They began to tiptoe toward the camp. Phil kept his eyes on the strangely built man, whose hatless head seemed very small on his long neck. He had narrow, sloping shoulders, and then he widened out in all directions down to his big hips.

While the man's back was still turned, Buzz and Kitsy caught their mother's eye. They both shook their heads, and Buzz held his finger over his mouth, hoping she would realize it was a signal not to talk. But Mrs. Fletcher misinterpreted. She thought they wanted to play a practical joke on the visitor. And to stave off embarrassment, she called out, "Oh, here they come now!"

"Doggone her!" Buzz muttered.

The stranger turned around to look at them. As he did so, a weird image crossed Phil's mind. The man looked exactly like a picture of a prehistoric dinosaur. His pinhead swung on his long neck, revealing a sloping forehead and a small chin, and between was a large nose that made his whole face seem to come to a point.

"Hello," the stranger said.

Phil and Buzz joined the circle standing near the fireplace. Kitsy stood back a little and kept shaking her head and frowning in her mother's direction. The stranger finished up a subject he had obviously been launched on. "Well, if you haven't used Tri-X film, you ought to get some. It will do wonders for your photographs when the light is poor." He paused. "I guess I'd better be going now."

Without more words, he climbed into his hardtop convertible Ford, waved good-bye, and drove cautiously out over the rutted road.

"What did that guy want?" Buzz asked urgently.

"He figured there was a campsite here and he was interested. We didn't invite him to share the fireplace, so I guess he decided to go someplace else," the Chief answered. "You know what, Amy, I think we ought to ask Boyd Blake to put a sign on the road saying 'Private.' We'll never get our work done if tourists keep following our tire tracks."

"Mom!" Buzz interrupted. "That guy is up to something! We caught him spying on our camp."

"What are you talking about?" the Chief demanded.

"When we got up to the Rustlers' Fort, we saw him sneaking off through the trees. Then when we came down, here he was. No fooling, you can see this place as plain as anything from the ledge." Buzz pointed up the hill.

Now that he knew what to look for, Phil could see the ledge through the shimmering tops of the aspen trees, and he thought he could even make out the wall of the fort.

"Funny, he didn't mention seeing you," the Chief said.

"Well, he probably thought *we* hadn't seen *him*," Phil

replied. "He was just sneaking away through the trees when we got there."

"Are you sure it's the same fellow?"

"Who could miss? He looks like a dinosaur," Phil said.

Buzz and Kitsy burst out laughing. "That's exactly what he looked like! A dinosaur!"

"Amy, he certainly was curious about our photographic equipment," the Chief exclaimed.

"Oh, Herbert! Are you going to be suspicious?"

"I don't like it, Amy. Remember, Mr. Post's fishing tackle box was stolen. I'm certainly going to ask Boyd Blake to put up a sign on our road saying 'Private.'"

"Herbert!"

"We saw him, and he was trying to sneak away," Kitsy said determinedly.

"Ye gods!" the Chief suddenly burst out. At that moment they could hear the sound of an engine. Somebody else was coming into camp. "This is just like Grand Central Station. When are we ever going to get any work done!"

A pickup truck belonging to the Park Service came into view and bounced confidently over the rough road. When it pulled up, Boyd Blake called, "Hi, there! I've got a present for the little lady. That is, if you agree—" He beamed at Kitsy, reached into the cab of the truck, and lifted out a spotted, yellowish furry bundle.

Kitsy gasped. "It's a kitten!"

"Did you ever see a kitten this big?" Boyd Blake asked. He stretched out the sleepy little animal. It was almost the size of a full-grown house cat. "It's a baby, all right—baby mountain lion. You can have it if you want it."

"*Felis concolor kaibabensis,*" the Chief said excitedly. "Where in the world did you get it?"

He reached out for the little animal and held it in his arms as if it were a baby while he examined it.

"Give it to me, Daddy. It's mine," Kitsy said.

In a moment she had squatted on the ground with the lion kitten on her lap.

"It's a sad story," Boyd Blake was explaining. "We found his mother had been killed by a tough old buck. It doesn't very often happen, but this time the lion apparently misjudged her opponent, and the buck's antlers stabbed her in the belly and she died. We found this little orphan near her, and somebody's got to bring it up on a bottle. It's lucky for us you're here. We don't want to lose any lions."

"What?" Phil asked. "Are lions valuable?"

"Sure," the Ranger answered. "The deer are increasing

too fast in the forest. If it weren't for the lions the deer would starve to death."

"That's like saying if it weren't for bank robbers the bankers would go broke," Phil laughed.

Blake grinned. "No, it's a fact. When you get too many deer, they eat up all the young trees. After a while there's no forest, and then all the deer starve to death. If there are enough mountain lions to eat part of the deer, the balance of nature is maintained."

Phil and Buzz squatted down beside Kitsy and began to stroke the lion kitten. The little animal reached up with its oversized paws to play with Phil's outstretched finger, then nipped him gently with its teeth.

"Dinnertime," Boyd Blake said, taking a baby's bottle from the pickup truck. "I brought along a case of canned milk and stuff to make his formula. Look, Mrs. Fletcher, you don't have to keep him, but I knew your husband was studying mountain lions—"

"You've won," Aunt Amy laughed.

Kitsy had the kitten flopped over her shoulder and was rubbing her cheek on its fur.

"You couldn't get it back even if you wanted it," the Chief added. "Kitsy is a natural-born zoo keeper. She likes anything with four feet and fur. She says she's going to be the kind of 'ologist' that takes care of animals."

"You don't have to be the least bit scared of him, Kitsy," the Ranger said. "If you're gentle with him, as I'm sure you will be, he'll make a perfect pet. Isn't that right, Chief? I ought to warn you, though, you'll have to give him back to us at the end of the summer. He's only about two weeks old now. When he's big enough to take care of himself, we'll turn him loose."

"Kitsy, did you hear that? You can have him all summer, but he has to stay here in the Park. This is his home."

"I know," Kitsy said. "Poor little orphan. I'm going to call him Oliver because he's an orphan. But I won't be mean to him the way people were to Oliver Twist."

"Another thing," Boyd Blake said, "he's so young you'll have to feed him every few hours for a while."

The Chief was suddenly worried. "Wait a minute, Boyd; I'm not sure we can keep him. We have trips to make, and we can't spend all our time kitten-sitting."

"No problem," said the Ranger cheerfully. "Any time you have to be away for any length of time you can leave what's-his-name—Oliver—with me. I brought along this cage, too. And here's a collar and a leash."

"Man, you thought of everything!" Phil laughed.

"Is it a deal?" Boyd Blake asked.

"Of course!" Kitsy said.

And her parents echoed her sentiments a little less enthusiastically.

With that, the Ranger hopped in the truck and started on his way before anybody had a chance for second thoughts. Then suddenly he slammed on his brakes, backed up, and asked, "Did you see a dog around here?"

"What kind of a dog?" Buzz asked.

"A big brown boxer. Some tourist lost him a couple of days ago. It's against the rules to let a dog off the leash in the Park, but this smart-aleck did, and the boxer ran away. If you find him, keep him until we can pick him up."

"What's his name?" Kitsy asked.

"Jack—maybe that's short for Jack Dempsey because he's a boxer," Boyd Blake joked. "His owner said he looks mean but is really as gentle as a lamb."

With a roar of the engine, Boyd Blake was gone.

Then the Chief remembered what he had meant to tell the Ranger: the suspicious behavior of the man in the business suit whom the kids called The Dinosaur, and the sign warning people that the road to their camp was private.

6

Phil watched Oliver sucking contentedly on the baby bottle that Kitsy held, and he had a sneaking desire to feed the little spotted mountain lion himself. But somehow he was afraid Kitsy would make fun of a fifteen-year-old boy who wanted to play nursemaid, so he didn't ask.

Apparently the same idea was going through Buzz's head. However, his desire to experiment overcame any fear of being laughed at.

"Give me a turn, Kitsy," Buzz said.

"All right," she agreed, a little unwillingly.

After Buzz had held the bottle for a while, Phil mustered up courage and took a turn. The lion kitten sucked greedily at first, with its two oversized forepaws on the bottle. Gradually it slowed down, and at last dropped off to sleep flat on its full tummy in Phil's lap. Now Kitsy exercised her rights of ownership. She lifted Oliver into her own lap and sat for a while admiring him as she leaned against the base of an aspen tree.

Then in the lengthening shadows of the late afternoon, she saw a deer approaching across the meadow.

"Here comes our doe," Aunt Amy said.

"How do you know it's the same one?" Phil demanded.

"I can tell by the scars on her side. She's been in some fight or other. Maybe another deer's horns or hoofs left those marks, or maybe a bobcat or even a lion clawed her."

Without a word, Kitsy rose and carried Oliver into the wall tent. In a minute she was back. Phil was ready to bet that Kitsy would have Oliver sleeping on her cot that night, no matter what her parents thought of the idea. Right now she had put Oliver out of sight, for fear the doe would see him and run away.

The doe trotted purposefully toward the camp; then as she drew near, she slowed down to a jerky walk. The next thing anyone knew she had seized a loaf of bread, which Aunt Amy had put on the table ready for supper, and began to eat it, paper and all.

"Hey!" Aunt Amy waved her dish towel at the animal.

"Mommy! You'll scare her," Kitsy wailed as the doe

bounded away and off into the woods.

"I wanted to, silly. Do you think I can let her eat up our supper?"

"I know, but we want her to get tame, don't we?"

The Chief looked up from something he was tinkering with on the tail gate of the station wagon. "I told you she'd be a pest, Amy. I've known her sort before, always dropping in for a free meal and prying into your business. Just like my Aunt Lulubelle."

"Herbert! Lulubelle was a very nice old lady. She was just lonesome."

"Lulubelle—that's it! That's going to be the deer's name. I've been trying to think," Kitsy exclaimed enthusiastically.

After supper Buzz surprised everyone by suddenly taking on the appearance of a man with a purpose in life. He rose from the table, scraped the dishes without being asked, then strode energetically over to the water faucet. There he attached the hose and started for the rear of his tent with the dishpan full of dirty plates and cups.

"What in the world are you doing, Buzz?" his mother asked.

"I'm going to put the Chief's hygienic public health device to good use. As the fellow on the radio says, housework can be a joy if you have efficient appliances."

Kitsy grinned. "He means he's going to wash the dishes under the shower."

While the Chief guffawed, his wife took a more serious view. "Oh, no you don't! Bring those dishes right back here, you scheming rascal. Cold water doesn't take the grease off," she said.

"Then I don't have to take any more showers?" Buzz said cheerfully.

"He's right, Aunt Amy," Phil put in. "If cold water doesn't take dirt off, what's the point of shower baths?"

"Come on, you two. Stop teasing me. There's hot water in the pot on the fireplace."

It was just getting dark, and the gasoline lantern had not yet been lit, when the boys finished the dishes. Some kind of commotion came from the upper end of the valley.

"I give up!" the Chief groaned. "Somebody else coming down that road! I'm going to have a barricade across it, if I have to put it there myself."

A few minutes later, a noisy group of boys and girls of college age swarmed into the meadow and came toward the dying campfire. One of them spied the Chief.

"Pardon me, sir, for bothering you," he said, "but our

car is stuck on the hill. I wonder if you could help us out."

"What are you coming down that road for in the first place?" the Chief demanded sharply.

"Why, we were planning to have a marshmallow roast. We didn't know anybody was camped here. We all work at the hotel."

"You see, Amy?" the Chief fumed. "We *have* to put a sign on the road." Then with a more friendly tone in his voice, he turned to the young man who was acting as spokesman for the group. "What seems to be your trouble?"

"The front end of our car dropped into a hole, and we're hung up. We can't move forward or back."

"Buzz, you get an ax," the Chief said. "Phil, you bring the shovel. Amy, you drive the station wagon. We'll go and see what we can do. Hurry up, hop in, Kitsy."

"I can't go," Kitsy said. "I have to stay and take care of Oliver."

"Oh, all right."

"It's time for you to go to bed, anyway, Kitsy," her mother said. "We'll be back soon."

The added manpower supplied by the Chief, Phil, and Buzz, plus the heaving and lifting done by the college kids, freed the old jalopy from the hole into which the front wheels had sunk. The picnickers backed up the road and went elsewhere for their marshmallow roast.

On the way back to camp, Phil said, "I don't see how they got stuck there. We never did."

"We never had about a dozen kids all stuffed into a jalopy that probably doesn't have any springs," the Chief reminded him. "I want you boys to go up with a shovel in the morning and make sure we can get out, though. It's too dark now to fix the road up."

As the station wagon stopped, its headlights revealed a strange sight. Kitsy was huddled under the heavy rustic camp table, clutching Oliver.

"Kitsy!" her mother cried. "What are you doing there?"

Slowly, Kitsy crept out from under the table. Her face was smeared with tears, and for a while she couldn't say anything. Her mother held her in her arms and asked, "Kitsy, dear, what's the matter? Did something frighten you?"

"Y-Y-Yes! There was a man here. I don't know what he was doing."

"Oh, Kitsy, it was probably Lulubelle," her mother said comfortingly. "Now, tell me exactly what happened."

Between sobs, Kitsy managed to get her story out. She

was just getting into bed when she heard a noise behind the tent. With Oliver in her arms, she stepped out to see what was making the noise. In the dusk she glimpsed the figure of a man close to the bushes that surrounded the shower bath. She was much too frightened to call for help, but she wanted to chase him away. With a sudden inspiration, she turned on the faucet and sent a flood of ice-cold water down on the intruder.

In spite of Kitsy's obvious distress, Phil and Buzz burst out laughing. Kitsy now mixed her own laughter with her sobs. "You should have heard him sputter!" she said. "And then he ran away."

"That's the second time Lulubelle had a bath today," the Chief said.

"It *wasn't* Lulubelle. It was a man!" Now Kitsy was angry at not being believed.

"I suspect it was one of those college boys," her mother said seriously. "They were all over the place."

"No, Mom. All the fellows were helping push their car out," Buzz said.

"How do we know?" Phil asked reasonably.

"I should have stayed in camp," Aunt Amy said. "They didn't even need the station wagon to push them out of the hole. I'm sorry, Kitsy. I shouldn't have gone and left you. But I really thought they might need me to push, while the menfolks lifted. You know how grateful we were to have somebody help us when we got stuck last year."

"Buzz! Turn off that shower!" The Chief's voice came from behind the tent.

Phil could see the Chief's flashlight searching the ground, and for the first time he realized that his uncle had said almost nothing during the excitement. The Chief must be taking Kitsy's report of an intruder very seriously.

The next morning, Phil was wakened by the sound of footsteps near his tent. He poked Buzz, and the two of them went out to see what was going on. The Chief stood near the shower, studying the meadow grass behind the tents, obviously looking for footprints.

"I can't make out anything," he said. The thick, wet grass was trampled, but the Fletcher party had all had showers yesterday, and no clear, fresh outlines of feet could show in the springy vegetation, anyway. The rocky hillside revealed no prints of boots or shoes, either.

"What do you think, Chief?" Phil asked.

"There's one fresh deer track. Amy may be right. It could have been Lulubelle or some other deer." The Chief pointed to a depression in one patch of mud that had been left by the shower water.

"That track was made after the shower was turned off," Phil said.

"Lulubelle could have been here twice," the Chief replied. Then he seemed to pull himself together. "Well, we can't waste any more time on speculation. After breakfast, you boys go up and fix the road. I want to see Boyd Blake, anyway, and I'll have to talk with him about the whole affair."

When Phil and Buzz reached the spot where the jalopy had been stuck the night before, they groaned at the job they would have to do. In the dark they hadn't seen clearly what had stopped the college boys' car. Now it was apparent that there was a deep hole in each rut. The front wheels of the car had sunk into the holes, and the high center in the road had made it impossible for the rear wheels to get traction.

"Gee, why didn't *we* ever get stuck here?" Buzz wondered.

"I guess the station wagon isn't as low-slung as that jalopy," Phil said.

"I bet we'd get stuck if we tried to drive up the road now," Buzz insisted.

"Sure, after all that digging and messing around we did last night."

"That's not what I mean. We didn't dig dirt out from *under* the front wheels last night. We threw dirt *in,* so as to lift them up," Buzz said emphatically.

"What are you trying to prove?" Phil asked.

"I think somebody made the ruts deeper on purpose," Buzz said slowly. "See those little piles of dirt? Somebody shoveled the dirt *out* of the ruts."

"Aw, nuts! Why would anybody do that? This road is bad enough already," Phil said impatiently.

"It would be a good way to cause us trouble. I tell you, Phil, something funny is going on around here. Mr. Post's fishing tackle box—The Dinosaur—the prowler last night —it all adds up."

"Adds up to what?" Phil wasn't trying to start an argument. He just didn't know. But he began to share his cousin's suspicions.

"I don't know exactly what it all amounts to, but it sure amounts to trouble. Come on, let's fill in the ruts so Pop can get out and tell the Rangers."

7

Before the Chief made his trip to Park headquarters, he laid out some jobs for Phil and Buzz. Kitsy and her mother spent most of the day across the meadow at the bird-watching station. When they strolled back toward camp in midafternoon, the boys had completed their work—and a project of their own besides.

"Did you get that tape recorder set up?" Aunt Amy asked.

"Yes, but please don't touch it," Buzz answered. "We want to show Pop when he comes back."

The tape recorder sat on the worktable, and on the ground beside it was the storage battery that would supply the electricity to run it. One of the boys' jobs had been to attach the wires to the battery and a transformer. Aunt Amy was going to use the machine to get records of bird songs. But in the meantime, the boys had found a use for it that they didn't want to advertise until the Chief returned.

Phil drew Kitsy to one side and enlisted her help in the plot. "Look, Kitsy, I can't explain now, but we've got a wonderful joke fixed up to play on the Chief, and you have to help."

Kitsy giggled. "That's fair. He's always playing jokes on us. What do you want me to do?"

"Buzz and I are going to take the shortcut, past the Rustlers' Fort, to the blacktop road. We'll wait for the Chief there. Then we'll ride home with him. The minute he stops the station wagon here at the camp, you switch on the tape recorder. I'll show you how. Don't tell your mother, and don't let her touch the tape recorder. That's all you have to do. Okay?"

"But what's the joke?" Kitsy demanded.

"You'll see. *Please,* Kitsy. Do just like I told you."

"Will it get me into trouble?"

"No! It'll be all right. I promise you."

"Okay," Kitsy agreed.

It was nearing the time when the Chief might return, so the two boys took off up the hill toward Rustlers' Fort.

As they approached it, both slowed their pace.

"Do you see anybody?" Phil whispered. He halfway expected to see The Dinosaur skulking near the fort.

"No," Buzz whispered back. "Shall we go on?"

"Sure. We have to."

They soon located the trail beyond the fort and went on to the blacktop road. When the station wagon came into view, Phil signaled ostentatiously, and the Chief stopped.

"What did Boyd Blake say?" Buzz asked.

"About what?" his father answered casually.

"About all the things that have been happening."

The Chief spluttered. "Oh, he said we were trying to make a monument out of a molecule. Those college kids work hard all day. They had the evening off, and they were in high spirits—wandering all over, getting stuck. One of them undoubtedly stumbled into our camp meaning no harm. However, Boyd did give me a sign."

As they turned off onto their dirt road, the Chief stopped. From the back of the station wagon they took a sawhorse on which was painted PRIVATE.

"This will stop 'em!" the Chief said with satisfaction as the boys put the sign in the middle of the dirt road.

Phil thought to himself that Boyd Blake's theory left several things unexplained. But they were drawing close to camp, and his attention was concentrated on Kitsy. Would she do the job she had promised to do?

Phil and Buzz lingered a moment in the front seat as the Chief hopped out.

"I'm going to turn on the radio, Pop, and get the news," Buzz announced. He made a motion toward the dashboard.

A moment later the camp was filled with sound:

"Flash! We interrupt this broadcast with the following bulletin: Phillip McKenney, rising young tennis star of Red Rock, Colorado, who disappeared from his home last week, has been located in an isolated spot in northern Arizona, where he is being exploited as a boy-slave of that mad scientist Herbert Q. X. R. Fletcher. Gaunt and wasted after only a week in the wilderness, young McKenney, according to our informant, may never be able to lift a tennis racquet again. 'Work, work,' McKenney said—"

"Who's done any work around here?" The Chief strode over and switched off the tape recorder. Then, imitating Buzz's imitation of a radio announcer, he intoned, "When interviewed in his cell in the Kanab jail, Herbert E. T. C. Fletcher had only this to say: 'When do we eat?' "

After supper the Chief went to the station wagon, let down the tail gate, and began to work by the light of a gasoline pressure lamp. Phil wandered over.

"What are you doing?" he asked.

"Making a sandwich for tomorrow." The Chief pointed to what looked like two huge slices of bread.

Phil was suspicious. He knew his uncle and his love of jokes. "Who's it for?" he asked.

"A mountain lion, I hope."

Phil looked closer at the slices and saw that they were chunks of cotton batting. "Quit kidding!" he said.

The Chief ignored him and set to work with an ice pick, punching holes in a rusty old pie plate. Phil watched without a word. His uncle glanced at him out of the corner of his eyes, grinned, said nothing, and kept on punching holes.

Phil decided to beat the Chief at his own game. "Um-hum!" he said wisely, nodding his head. He looked closer and noticed that the Chief seemed to be making the holes in a regular pattern that formed letters. s-n-i-f-f was on one line. Below it the letters h-e-r-e slowly emerged.

Solemnly Phil leaned over, sniffed, then walked away.

"Hey, what are you two up to?" called Buzz who had been watching the performance.

Phil turned to his uncle. "I don't know. Do you?"

The Chief grinned and answered, "You'll find out tomorrow." After that he checked over his camera equipment. Plainly he was going to keep on teasing.

Buzz motioned to Phil and drew him away under the trees. "Listen," he said. "We'll get even with Pop for being so mysterious. That tape recorder is still rigged up on the worktable. If we turn it on after he goes to sleep, we'll have scientific evidence of the night noises made by that rare animal *Herbertus Fletcherensis*. Then just let him tell us he doesn't snore!"

"Buzz, you deserve a medal!" Phil chuckled.

"Come on, let's pretend we're going to bed now."

"Don't be a dope," Phil said. "We have to sit around the campfire for a while, so we don't look suspicious."

Phil took a stick and lifted up the iron grate from the top of the fireplace, then heaped on some wood. Soon a fine fire was blazing up. The Chief finishing his puttering and Aunt Amy got the last of the food stowed away so that night animals couldn't steal it. Kitsy came out of the tent and reported that Oliver was sound asleep after another meal. Then the five of them sat cross-legged on the ground around the fire. They were glad for its warmth.

A mood of security and comfort gave Phil a good feeling. There was something special about camping out and sitting around like this at the end of the day.

The Chief broke the silence. "Tomorrow we'll get ready for the lion, kids. Boyd Blake says one of its feet has only three toes. When the Rangers were building this campsite, they saw its tracks on top of the ridge over there. It could be that old Three-Toes is sitting close by in the dark watching us right now. These big American cats are very curious about people."

An involuntary shiver went through Phil. Was there any chance that a lion would jump out at them?

"One time," the Chief went on, "I was sitting by the campfire, just like this, up in the mountains in Colorado. I happened to turn around, and there he was—a big cat, crouched on a log, staring at me. The log made a natural bridge over the creek beside our camp, and he'd come halfway across it to investigate."

"Weren't you scared, Daddy?" Kitsy asked.

"I guess I have to admit I was a little scared," her father replied. "Actually there are only a few cases on record in which a mountain lion has attacked a human being. But it has happened, and nobody claims the records are complete.

Even the lions that have been tamed can go bad."

"You mean Oliver might be dangerous?" Phil asked.

"No, Oliver's much too small. He'll be perfectly safe, at least until he gets big enough to catch his own raw meat. Some lions have made perfect pets all their lives."

"Tell them about that one up in Montana, Herbert," said Aunt Amy.

"Oh, yes, there was a fellow in a mining camp who adopted a kitten like Oliver. Then he trained it to pull a little cart. It was one of the sights of the town to see him driving up the center of the main street, hauled along in the cart by a full-grown puma."

"Puma?" Phil said.

"Yes, these big cats have lots of names—puma, cougar, panther, painter, mountain lion. It's the same animal, but they call it different things in different places."

"How big will Oliver get?" Kitsy asked.

"No telling. He might weigh a hundred and fifty or two hundred pounds. Teddy Roosevelt killed one that weighed two hundred and twenty-seven pounds and was eight feet long from the tip of his nose to the tip of his tail. They've found them even bigger than that."

"Is jaguar another name for mountain lion?" Phil asked.

"No, that's a different cat altogether," the Chief answered. "Even bigger. In ancient times jaguars used to roam over most of the United States, but now you only see them down along the Mexican border. A jaguar is spotted all his life, the way Oliver is now. But Oliver will lose his spots as he grows up. He'll probably be a tawny color that will blend in with the trees and rocks where he lives."

"Okay, children, time to go to bed," Aunt Amy said. "We have a big day tomorrow."

Buzz hadn't forgotten the snore-recording project. He nudged Phil and the two of them dutifully went to their tent, after looking briefly to make sure that the tape recorder was still on the worktable.

One of the things Phil liked best about camping out with the Fletchers was that everybody went to bed in the clothes he had on, taking off only shoes and socks—if he thought about them. Aunt Amy didn't make you change until the next morning when you took your shower in cold spring water.

Now in the dark tent Phil and Buzz lay on their sleeping bags, listening intently for the sounds which they wanted to record. Phil began to grow drowsy, and to keep awake he whispered to Buzz, "What do you really think about that Dinosaur fellow?"

"Gee, I almost forgot about him," Buzz answered.

"He sure was spying on this place," Phil said thoughtfully. "And he was nosy as all get out when he was talking to your folks."

A sudden burst of giggles came from the wall tent. Apparently Oliver had done something that amused Kitsy.

"Won't they ever go to sleep?" Buzz said in disgust.

But Phil was still on The Dinosaur. "Aside from looking funny he acted funny," he said.

"Who?"

"The Dinosaur, who else? I'll bet he was the one that took Mr. Post's fishing tackle box."

Buzz sat up again. "You could be right. Maybe we had better put the tape recorder away—when we're through with it."

They remained silent for a while. Then Phil poked Buzz and whispered, "It's all quiet over there."

Both listened intently. "We better wait a couple more minutes. Pop doesn't always fall asleep in a hurry."

They sat, hugging their knees, waiting. Then, a sound caught Phil's ear. Another—and another. He leaned over and whispered, "Do you hear that? What is it?"

"Footsteps!"

Both of them were rigid with tension and fear. The soft stealthy noises continued: a few steps, then a pause, then a few more and another pause.

Phil knew he should do something, but he couldn't make a muscle work for a while. Finally, mustering all his courage, he moved forward on hands and knees and put his head slowly out through the door of the tent. The long wait in the darkness had accustomed his eyes to the night. The Chief had covered the fire with dirt before he turned in, and it gave no light, but Phil could make out the dim outlines of the wall tent and the fireplace. Not a moving thing was in sight. He listened. The footsteps had stopped.

Suddenly a terrifying crash broke the silence of the night. Then came the sound of running. Before he knew what he was doing, Phil had sprung to his feet and leaped out of the tent. In a second the Chief was out with a flashlight. And there, disappearing across the meadow, Phil saw a deer— probably Lulubelle.

The Chief swung his light around till it fell on the big Park Service garbage can. The can lay on its side with the lid off. Lulubelle had tipped it over.

"Drat that deer! We'll never have any peace. And drat the boy who didn't put the lid on tight. She smelled those honeydew melon rinds and was trying to get a meal. From now on, whoever has his turn at cleaning up has to be sure the lid is *on*."

Shamefaced, Phil, who was the guilty party, set the garbage can up and made sure it was tightly closed.

It seemed like hours before the Chief calmed down.

"Didn't you think it was The Dinosaur?" Phil asked Buzz as they lay waiting on their sleeping bags again.

"I guess I did," Buzz admitted. "Anyway, the more I think about him the less I like him."

After another silence, Buzz whispered, "If you don't talk about something, I'm going to fall asleep. I can hardly keep my eyes open."

"All right. Let's talk about our Geiger counter. Are you still willing to put up two dollars and borrow nine from me?"

"I guess so . . . . Yeah, sure." Buzz revived a little.

"We can carry it along on trips when we go with the Chief and use it when he's not looking. It will sure be a good joke on him when we find some uranium. There has to be some here. It's all over this part of the Southwest."

"What's that?" Buzz interrupted.

Phil listened.

"Eureka! The Chief's snoring at last. Here we go."

The boys crept out of the tent and over to the table on which the tape recorder sat. Inside the wall tent, all was silence except for the snorts and gurgles that came from the Chief in a rhythmic sequence growing louder and louder. Then there would be a moment of silence followed by a soft grunt, and the racket would begin to mount again. Carefully, noiselessly Buzz raised the lid of the recorder box. Just at the point when the snorts grew loudest, Buzz turned on the switch. Luckily the noise of the running machinery seemed to blend with the slight rustle of the wind in the aspen trees. In the tiny light that came up from the recorder, the boys looked at each other and grinned. Everything had gone off perfectly.

They eased themselves into chairs at the worktable and rested their heads on their arms, leaning forward. This had to be a good long recording to prove their point. The low droning hum of the machine lulled them. Phil knew he ought to poke Buzz to keep him awake. But the effort seemed too much. He would do it in just a minute . . . . But Phil himself fell asleep.

The scream that woke him set him on his feet as if he had been shocked with electricity. It came again, and then again. The most horrible sound he had ever heard. A woman was in great pain—being murdered—but who—and where?

Buzz stumbled to his feet and knocked the chair over.

"Who's that?" came the Chief's voice from inside the tent.

"Us!" Phil gasped.

"What's the matter, Daddy? What's the matter?" Kitsy cried.

"What's the trouble, boys?" the Chief asked sharply as he came to the tent door.

"Didn't you hear?" Buzz whispered. "It's awful. Somebody's getting killed."

"You're imagining things. You had a nightmare."

"We did not!" Buzz whispered. "Listen."

They all kept quiet. The Chief heard nothing but a strange humming noise. With his flashlight he looked around. The tape recorder was still spinning.

"What does this mean?" he barked.

Kitsy and her mother were out of the tent by now.

"I don't think this kind of thing is very funny," the Chief said sternly. "Trying to scare us and wake us up this way.

You boys are too old for that. I'm ashamed of you. We'll discuss this tomorrow morning. Now, to bed with you."

He reached out and flipped off the recorder.

"Listen, Chief! Listen to me!" Phil said desperately. "Something is wrong around here. We did hear a scream."

"Herbert," Aunt Amy said, "I thought I was dreaming, but I believe I did hear a strange noise."

"If there was any noise, it's on there," Kitsy said, pointing to the tape recorder.

"That's right!" Buzz exclaimed.

With the aid of a flashlight, he found the knobs and reversed the ribbon. A few moments later, peculiar noises began to come out.

"Something's wrong with that machine," the Chief grumbled.

In spite of their fear, the boys could not contain themselves. "It's working just fine!" Buzz chortled.

"Is that what scared you?" the Chief demanded.

"No! That's you snoring!" Buzz exploded.

His mother's laugh broke out like a clear, soothing peal of music in the night that had been so troubled. The monotonous rhythmic rise and fall of snoring went on.

"Shut that thing off," the Chief ordered.

"We can't," Phil protested. "You gotta wait till the scream comes. We went to sleep. We don't know how long you snored. Wait!"

The Chief began pacing around in the dark, spluttering and fuming. Then he stopped in his tracks as a weird scream came from the recorder. It didn't sound as close and loud as it had when Phil first heard it, but it was there. Again he felt his flesh creep, and alarm swept over him.

"See!" Buzz cried.

"We've got to *do* something!" Phil whispered.

There was another scream from the machine.

"That's it! That's it!" The Chief was now more excited than anybody. "Nobody ever got it before. This is wonderful!"

"Chief! Talk sense!" Phil exclaimed.

His uncle was now leaning over the machine. He wound the tape back a little way and listened to the terrible sounds again. Finally he straightened up. By now Aunt Amy had the gasoline pressure lamp going.

"Boys, you have been the first to record the famous mating call of *felis concolor kaibabensis.*"

"He means the mountain lion," Kitsy said and started off to bed.

8 THREE-TOES AND HIS KILL

"Up and at 'em!" the Chief called the next morning.

Phil and Buzz, who had had a very short night's sleep as a result of their tape-recording experiment, groaned and turned over.

"Come on, you loafers!"

Phil opened his eyes. This was the day—the day he'd been looking forward to. He was actually going to take part in the search for a mountain lion. The warm, comfortable lethargy of sleep suddenly disappeared. He was wide awake. But now that the hunt was about to start, he had mixed feelings. He had never heard anything so awful as the scream of that lion in the night. The fear it had roused in him still lingered.

"Hey! If you boys don't hurry, Kitsy will give your oatmeal to Lulubelle!" the Chief shouted.

"No fair!" Buzz shouted back. He was out of the tent and in his seat at the camp table with a speed that was amazing for him.

His mother took the oatmeal pot off the table, put it back on the gasoline stove, and with the spoon in her hand pointed meaningfully at the shower.

"Aw, Ma! Well—all right."

Soon Buzz and Phil were spluttering and yowling with the shock of the cold water.

"Bring on your lion!" Phil yelled exuberantly while he rubbed himself dry. Now he felt ready for anything. In no time, he was dressed.

Running toward the camp table, he passed Kitsy who sat wrapped up in a blanket in her father's folding chair, giving Oliver his breakfast. She had slept with his bottle next to her all night to keep it warm.

"Kitsy, what did Oliver have to say about those screams last night?" Phil asked.

"He didn't hear them," Kitsy answered. "Our heads were under the covers."

Phil had a sudden image of the horror his mother would feel at the idea of taking a kitten—let alone a mountain lion kitten—to bed. He had never before realized that two closely related families could have such different ideas about what kids should be allowed to get away with.

After the boys had consumed second bowls of oatmeal and cups of hot chocolate, the Chief began to swing into action. Phil and Buzz brought their knapsacks and stuffed into them the various pieces of gear that the Chief distributed.

"You two ladies take good care of camp," he said to his wife and Kitsy as he and the boys turned to trudge across the meadow. "We should be back by noon."

"Good luck," Aunt Amy called after them.

The woods all around their meadow rang with early morning bird songs. Phil had never realized before how much music there was in the forest and how many different tones and notes and scales there were in the orchestra of nature. He began to understand why Aunt Amy wanted to record all this on tape. And what a difference there was between morning sounds and the horrifying screech that had split the air during the night!

As the three of them left the meadow and entered the woods, Phil's earlier burst of confidence about searching for the lion began to wane. He glanced around at the trees and rocks that might offer hiding places for a big cat, and he wasn't at all sure he wanted to encounter Three-Toes. Once more it occurred to him that his uncle was a little foolhardy in not having a gun along for protection. The kind of animal that could make the awful sounds he had heard only a few hours before would think nothing of tearing a human being—or two or three—to bits. Still, he was determined not to show his fear. He followed briskly after the Chief who was angling up along the rugged hillside.

Before long the Chief announced, "We're almost up to the saddle. That's supposed to be a kind of low pass that leads to the head of a canyon on the other side of the ridge. Boyd Blake told me that the saddle is a kind of station for old Three-Toes. He passes by here about every twenty days. Let's all begin to keep our eyes open for tracks."

Phil had no idea what the tracks of a lion would look like, but he scanned the ground—between glances to the right and the left. He simply couldn't get out of his mind the thought that Three-Toes might be lurking nearby, ready to pounce.

"Zuleika! as Archimedes said to Dr. Watson!" the Chief suddenly exclaimed with immense satisfaction. He pointed at the ground. Phil looked over the area indicated by the Chief's finger. "There—and there!"

The Chief touched a little mound of gravel with his boot toe. Phil could see, scattered here and there, what looked like small bundles of hair, and he said so.

"That's just what they are," the Chief said, "deer's hair that has passed through the stomach of a mountain lion. This place is what we call a scratch hill. Lions are very neat creatures. They always bury their droppings in scratch hills, and they often use the same area time and time again."

Amazed, Phil looked and saw several more small heaps of gravel he hadn't noticed before.

"These show that a mountain lion has made many trips past this place, but there's no *fresh* scratch hill. That means he hasn't been here lately. So, we'll fix his sandwich for him. There's a good chance that he'll be along soon, to judge by that meowing we heard last night."

A meow was the last thing in the world the screech had sounded like, but Phil didn't care to argue the point. If there was work to do, he wanted to do it and get away.

The Chief studied the trees nearby. "That one over there will be about right for the sandwich," he said. "Open up your knapsacks."

Out came the two slabs of cotton batting, the old rusty pie plate in which he had been making the holes last night, and a small jar that Phil hadn't seen before.

"What are you up to, anyway?" Phil asked.

"We're going to make Three-Toes take a picture of himself. First we clamp my other camera to that tree." The Chief indicated a small aspen. "Then we'll fix a place for him to step on so that he'll snap the picture. And finally, we have to make sure that he steps exactly where we want him to step."

After some measuring for distance, the Chief took from his knapsack a box that was painted an inconspicuous gray-brown—a waterproof case that held a camera with a flash attachment. In no time, it was clamped securely around the aspen. The lens was focused toward a large fir tree.

Next, with a little trenching shovel, the Chief dug a shallow hole in front of the fir tree and put into it a queer-looking gadget.

"What's that?" Buzz asked.

"An electric switch that will set the camera off," his father answered. "When Three-Toes puts his weight on the switch, he will complete an electric circuit—there are batteries in that camera box. The electric current will do two things at once. It will activate a magnet that clicks the shutter, and in the same instant it'll set off the flash bulb. I have to use flash because there's a lot of shade here. Besides, Three-Toes might come at night."

"That's neat!" Phil exclaimed.

"How do you know he'll trip the switch?" Buzz asked.

"That's where the sandwich comes in," the Chief explained. "You can fix it. Open that little jar. There's a kind of paste in it. Spread the paste on one piece of cotton; then put the other piece on top."

"First Lulubelle eats paper and now lions eat cotton!" Phil shook his head in perplexity. He opened the jar, and the paste inside gave off a pungent odor. Then he glanced at the pie plate in which his uncle had spelled out SNIFF HERE with the holes he had punched in it. Phil was beginning to get the idea, and so was Buzz.

"Pop, how do you know this lion can read?" Buzz asked.

The Chief had been using a hand ax to chop a rough circle in the bark of the fir tree. "We've got something here that's in the language everyone can understand."

"I should have known it!" Phil said. The odor of the paste had been rousing some memory in his mind. Now he saw an image of his own cat at home playing with a small bag—a catnip bag! "No fooling! Do mountain lions go for catnip, too?"

"Absolutely. They can't leave the stuff alone," the Chief answered. "The minute they smell it they go up to the sandwich and stand there sniffing for a long time."

By now he had a flat round surface just the size of the pie plate chopped out of the bark of the fir tree a couple of feet above the ground where the switch had been set. The Chief took the catnip sandwich and put it in the plate. Then he nailed the whole thing snugly against the tree, with the cotton inside.

"The pitch from the tree will help to keep the cotton moist," he said, "and that will keep the smell of the bait fresh, and the plate protects the sandwich."

"I still don't see how you can get Three-Toes to step on the switch," Phil said. "He could sniff the sandwich and never once put a foot where you want him to."

The Chief took out of his knapsack a piece of canvas stretched on a circular frame and placed it over the switch. Then he covered the canvas lightly with earth. Obviously this was a flexible protection for the switch mechanism.

"Lions watch where they step," the Chief was answering Phil's question at last. "They never set foot on a twig in their travelway, if they can help it. They step on bare ground or stone wherever they can." As he talked, he made a design of twigs all around the base of the fir tree. The arrangement looked haphazard, but if a lion wanted to sniff the catnip, he would have to step on the bare earth that covered the switch. A wire that connected the switch to the camera ran unobtrusively over the ground.

"That does it!" the Chief said with satisfaction, after he had inspected the whole layout. "Mr. Three-Toes will do the rest—I hope. Now we might as well get going."

Phil and Buzz shouldered their knapsacks.

"We'll see if we can trace this travelway back in the direction of camp. If we keep our eyes open, we might even catch a glimpse of Three-Toes." The Chief in the lead walked very slowly. He wanted to be sure at every point that he was on the trail used by the lion. Phil loved activity and this hiking at a snail's pace began to get on his nerves. More and more he thought about what would happen if they *should* meet the lion. Several times he looked questioningly at Buzz, wondering if his cousin shared his own misgivings. But their pace seemed to suit Buzz, who was never in a hurry, anyway, and he was as much absorbed in studying the travelway and peering into the woods on either side as his father was. Phil envied his calm.

The travelway seemed to be a natural path through the

sparse underbrush, although Phil probably wouldn't have noticed that there was any particular trail if it hadn't been pointed out to him. At a small clearing the Chief stopped.

"You know what I think?" he said. "I believe the travel-way and the old horse thieves' trail are one and the same, for a long way. This is the natural route in and out of Dry Bones Canyon. But look, right here the trail divides. The rustlers started downhill from this point, but the lion keeps on along the ridge."

Phil looked out across an open space that lay far below. That must be where their camp was. And there on the opposite ridge stood Rustlers' Fort. The Chief decided to keep on a little farther.

"What's that?" Phil pointed to a heap of freshly turned-up earth. Sticking out of the dirt were the head and fore-legs of a doe. It looked as if a haphazard attempt had been made to bury the carcass.

"Don't scuff up the ground, boys," the Chief ordered. "I want to get some pictures."

"What happened?" Phil asked uncertainly. It was a shock to see the body of a big animal, and strange to see it half-buried.

As the Chief focused his camera, he answered absentmindedly, "Lion killed it. He had a big meal from it and then covered it up. Lions often do that."

Phil followed his uncle and studied the paw prints he was now photographing.

"It must be Three-Toes!" Phil burst out. "There's a toe missing!"

Most of the prints showed a pad with four toes in a semicircle around it, but in some prints there was an unmistakable gap.

"It's Three-Toes, all right," the Chief agreed. "And he killed this doe only a short time ago." Now he straightened up and looked into the woods all around. "I wouldn't be surprised if he's close by somewhere, sleeping off his big breakfast. Maybe when he's hungry he'll come back for another meal. Lions sometimes do that."

"Shouldn't we get out of here?" Phil asked, and he couldn't keep the nervousness from his voice. "He might get sore if he saw us monkeying around his meat."

"It's too bad we didn't set the camera trap here," Buzz said. Apparently he was convinced there was no real danger.

"No, it's not at all certain he'll come back to this place," the Chief answered. "He may want fresh meat when he gets hungry again."

"There's plenty of it around," Buzz remarked.

Phil glanced at the other two suspiciously. Were they talking about deer, or were they slyly kidding about the meat on their own bones? He cast an uneasy glance behind him, then all around. Downhill to the right he thought he saw something. He looked again.

Half hidden by scrawny, low plants lay an object that seemed to have brown hair glistening in a little patch of sunlight. Was he just seeing things? Would the Chief or Buzz make fun of him if he mentioned it? It was just the color he thought a lion would be.

Phil forced himself to whisper a warning. "Chief, what is that over there?" He gestured with his head, somehow fearing that if he raised his arm and pointed, the motion might provoke an attack.

The Chief showed alertness in every bit of his small, lean body. After a long, silent look he relaxed and said, "Whatever it is, it's not our friend Three-Toes—I'm sorry to say." Decisively he walked straight toward it.

Both boys held back until they heard the Chief say, "Oh-oh, this is too bad. Stay there a minute. I want to try and figure something out."

He bent over and methodically surveyed the ground,

working back toward the carcass of the deer.

"What is it, Pop?" Buzz demanded.

"All right, now you can go have a look, and I'll tell you what I think," the Chief answered.

Phil and Buzz went toward the patch of brown hair. It belonged to the lifeless body of a big, brown boxer dog.

"That must be the dog Boyd Blake told us about," Phil said. "The lion must have killed it." He leaned over and peered at the animal's collar which bore a brass plate with the name "Jack" on it. "It is. It's that dog. Gee, too bad!"

"Maybe he tried to steal some of Three-Toes' dinner, and Three-Toes lit into him," Buzz suggested.

"That might be, but I doubt it," the Chief said. "There's something about this I don't understand. From the looks of the tracks, I'd swear that the dog attacked while Three-Toes was covering up his kill. It's a mighty strange house pet that will do that. I can't figure out why the dog would have attacked."

After a silence, the Chief pulled himself together. "Well, if Three-Toes is anywhere around here, he's seen us—and that means we won't see him." He looked at his wrist watch.

"I don't need that to tell me I want to go home," Buzz

said. "I've got a dandy alarm clock right between my gizzard and my gullet."

"Okay, let's go." The Chief was full of cheer. As far as he was concerned, the long morning's work had been a complete success.

But Phil was more upset than satisfied. He had felt frightened so many times this morning that he wondered if he was really "chicken." Nobody had ever called him that. In a basketball game or in a tennis match where there were opponents whom he could see, he always put up a good fight. But ever since he had arrived on the North Rim, peculiar things had been happening. There seemed to be dangers and threats and unexplained happenings. His uncle's obvious bewilderment at finding the dead boxer somehow returned Phil to questions he had had about a lot of other things—The Dinosaur, the prowler who had frightened Kitsy, the strange holes in the road that had stopped the college kids—lots of things.

Phil was glad when he got back to camp where a big pot of soup was steaming over the fire. He ate in silence while Buzz and the Chief reported the morning's events. Darned if he would let this place get him down, he decided. And immediately he began to feel better.

9 **TROUBLE IN THE MOONLIGHT**

After lunch, Kitsy sat with Oliver in her lap and watched the boys suffering. She had done her laundry that morning while they were out trailing the lion. Now Aunt Amy had insisted that Phil and Buzz had to wash their clothes *and* clean out their tent.

"I don't understand," she said, "why neither one of you can think of putting your dirty socks in the laundry bag, instead of sleeping with them. Your tent is a mess."

"But, Ma, we've been busy," Buzz protested.

"I know. Well, get busy again and do your wash. The quicker you finish it, the more time you'll have to yourself the rest of the afternoon."

Phil dutifully collected his share of the socks but left those which belonged to Buzz just where they had been dropped. There wasn't any way to get out of the chore.

Suddenly he remembered the pair of his jeans that still showed the marks of his encounter with Lulubelle their first night in the Park. His leg was well now, but he still hated to let the elder Fletchers know that he had foolishly disobeyed instructions. When he thought no one was looking he poured half a bottle of bleach into a bucket and put the torn jeans in to soak, hoping that he could get rid of the bloodstains in a hurry.

"What you doing, dopey?" Kitsy asked. "You'll take all the color out of your pants!"

Phil looked up innocently. "I thought you always used bleach when you washed things." All the while he was busily sloshing and scrubbing on the jeans.

"Oh, Phil!" Aunt Amy exclaimed.

"Too late now," Phil said in a cheery voice. "Besides white pants are fashionable." Working rapidly, he rubbed the stains under the water to remove the signs of his crime before his aunt got suspicious.

Finally the whole wash was done, and the boys hung it on a clothesline rigged between two trees. Phil's once-blue jeans were conspicuous with streaks and blotches of white. They were not things of beauty. Nevertheless, he had a sense of achievement. He had never done his own laundry before, and it somehow gave him the feeling that he was beginning to make good as a camper.

Buzz had no such noble thought. "Now," he said gloomily to his mother, "can we go and *do* something?"

She ignored him and said to Phil, "Have you written a decent letter to your mother and father? I seem to remember you haven't sent anything but postcards."

Phil groaned. The day was a dead loss. Buzz, he noticed, was quietly disappearing around the back of the wall tent.

"Oh, no, you don't," Aunt Amy called. "Buzz, you *have* to clean up that tent."

Buzz thought a minute, then grinned mischievously. "Okay," he said, "if I can turn on the tape recorder and listen to that mountain lion scream while I work."

While Phil struggled with the letter, Buzz insisted on playing the tape over and over, beginning at the beginning, with the long and monotonous record of his father's snores. The Chief had been sitting in his chair, writing in a notebook. At last he jumped up and shouted, "How long do I have to listen to that blasted nonsense, Amy?"

"Sorry, Herbert," she answered. "It's my fault. I told Buzz he could play the machine. Why don't you stop working for a while and take a walk with me? I'd like to show you a grosbeak's nest I found in the woods this morning."

Grumbling, the Chief went off with his wife, and the boys turned the tape recorder on even louder. It was so loud that it almost drowned out another sound—the roar of Boyd Blake's pickup truck approaching camp.

"Hi," the Ranger said to Kitsy.

"Hi! I'm teaching Oliver tricks." She dangled an aspen branch above the lion kitten who tried clumsily to stand on his hind legs and bat at the elusive leaves.

At that moment the piercing scream of the mountain lion came from the tape recorder. The Ranger stiffened. Phil and Kitsy burst out laughing, then quickly explained.

"This is wonderful!" Blake exclaimed. "I'll have to borrow the tape when I give my next talk to the tourists."

"You can't have it unless you promise to play all of it, including Pop's snores," said Buzz who had come out of the tent. "You could call your talk 'Noted Naturalist Sleeps Through Lion Attack.' "

"Don't ever think I won't," the Ranger answered, laughing. "Well, so long. I was driving by, and it occurred to me I might as well see how your baby is doing."

Blake was ready to leave when Phil remembered to tell him about the boxer and the fresh sign of old Three-Toes.

"Too bad about the boxer. I'll write a letter to its owner, and thanks. Tell your folks I'll be back to borrow that tape recording."

All through dinner the Chief protested that he couldn't possibly lend the recording to the Park Naturalist. "None of you realize what an extraordinary thing we have here," he said soberly. "It's too valuable to let out of my possession. This is unique. Nobody has ever recorded the lion's purr *and* his scream, too."

"Purr?" Phil asked.

"What are you talking about?" said Buzz.

"Why, you recorded ten minutes or so of that deep, contented purr before the scream goes on. Every zoo and natural history museum in the country will want to hear it."

Kitsy giggled. "Daddy, when you snore you do sound just like Oliver purring, only about five times louder."

"Snores!" he grunted.

"Chores, you mean," Aunt Amy said. "Herbert, it's your turn to do the dishes."

With a great rattling of plates and pans and knives and forks, the Chief set to work. He rolled up his sleeves and was about to plunge his hands into the dishwater when Kitsy yelled, "Daddy! You're forgetting your watch again."

"Kitsy," the Chief said solemnly as he removed his watch, "why did the little moron take the alarm clock to bed with him?"

"I don't know. Why?"

"Because he'd heard that pillows were supposed to have ticking on them."

"Oooh!" Buzz groaned.

"Daddy," Kitsy came back at her father, "why did the little moron throw his watch into the Grand Canyon?" Then she answered her own question before anyone else had a chance. "Because he wanted to see time fly."

"Oh-ooh!" Buzz groaned again.

"That reminds me," Aunt Amy said. "We've been here nearly a week and haven't driven out to Cape Royal to see the view. If you boys pitch in and help Herbert with the dishes, we'll be able to get there before the moon goes down. And the canyon by moonlight must be wonderful."

"If we help you now, will you help us tomorrow, Chief?" Buzz asked.

"It's a deal," the Chief agreed cheerfully.

In no time the camp was slicked up, and they all piled into the station wagon. Kitsy held Oliver in her lap. She was convinced that he was too little to be left alone.

The forest looked very different by moonlight, as they wound around the countless curves of the road, and everyone enjoyed in silence the strange effects created by silver streaks of light breaking through the black wall of trees. Phil discovered that he was unconsciously counting the deer that leaped away or simply stood watching them. Once a buck halted in the road, confused by the glare of the headlights, and they had to stop and wait till he bounded off into the trees. By the time they reached the parking area at Cape Royal, where tourists had to leave their cars, Phil had seen eighteen bucks and does. Strange how most deer seemed to appear only at night and remain hidden during the day. For some reason, Lulubelle and a few others didn't keep such regular hours.

Zipping up their jackets, the boys walked through the chilly evening wind, out toward the edge of the Canyon. All of a sudden, Phil realized that he was on the edge of nothing. Only an iron rail stood between him and a vast jagged emptiness that stretched endlessly below. His two hands grabbed for the rail with convulsive strength, and at the same time his body drew back. His stomach felt hollow. It was several moments before he could relax enough to look beyond the rail. The dim shapes of rock pinnacles and cliffs shone in the moonlight and stood out against the dead black of the shadows. No telling how far it was from any one place to another. He had never seen anything so immense, and so terrifying. When he had had his first glimpse of the Canyon by daylight, it had filled him with awe and curiosity. But now it seemed forbidding and too eerie and strange to be part of this world.

No one wanted to stay long. It was cold and somehow exhausting to know that on three sides of you, as you stood at the end of the rock point, cliffs dropped away below for hundreds of feet. Back at the station wagon, Phil felt a sudden warm sense of security. "Whew!" he said. "I don't mind admitting that place scares me."

"I know what you mean, Phil," Aunt Amy said. "It's both terrible and wonderful, isn't it?"

But Kitsy said flatly, "I don't like it."

"You'll get used to it," her father assured her. "A lot of things are scary until you learn about them. You'll feel differently after you've been all the way down to the bottom of the Canyon and back. You'll get the idea you can lick a place like this, even if it is the biggest hole in the world."

This idea appealed to Phil. He liked the thought that there was a chance to come out on top in a contest with this great, wild canyon country. But almost immediately something happened that broke his mood of returning confidence. As the station wagon pulled to a stop back in the campground, he saw a moving figure just disappearing out of the moonlight, which still spilled down on their camp, into the impenetrable shade of the trees behind. His reason told him that it was Lulubelle, but his imagination said it might be a human prowler.

Aunt Amy obviously saw the same thing. "There goes that rascally Lulubelle," she said. "I hope we didn't leave anything around for her to get into."

"No campfire tonight," the Chief announced. "It's time for bed."

"What time *is* it?" Buzz demanded.

"It's—hey, Amy!" the Chief spluttered. "Where's my watch? I left it right here on the table while I was doing the dishes, and then you rushed us away so fast I forgot to put it on."

The beam of his flashlight showed clearly that there was no watch on the table and no watch under it—no watch to be found anywhere.

"Do you suppose Lulubelle tried to eat it?" Buzz asked.

"Certainly not!" his father answered irritably. "That

watch has a metal wristband. A deer might lick a leather band for the salt on it, but she wouldn't chew on metal. Are any of you playing a trick on me? If you are, I want you to tell me right now."

"Oh, Herbert, it's around here someplace. You'll find it in the morning," Aunt Amy said.

But Phil began to wonder. "Aunt Amy, maybe that wasn't Lulubelle we saw when we drove into camp," he said. "Maybe it was somebody who—"

"Nonsense! We'll find the watch," Aunt Amy interrupted. "Herbert's always misplacing things, and they always turn up later."

"I didn't *mis*place that watch. I *placed* it right here," the Chief said firmly.

"Oh, Herbert!" she exclaimed. And just to prove that there had been no thief around, she went into the wall tent and checked over all the equipment. Everything was in its place, undisturbed.

"See, nobody's been bothering things," Aunt Amy said. "Herbert, I tell you it will turn up. Things like that always do. Now let's go to bed."

As Phil lay in his sleeping bag, trying to relax, he wasn't at all sure that his aunt was right.

10   "WATCH OUT FOR THE WATCH!"

"What the dickens is wrong with your father!" Phil nudged Buzz as the two boys emerged from their tent the next morning.

The sight that greeted them was most extraordinary. There sat the Chief at the table, which was already laid out for breakfast, staring as if in a trance at a large whole grapefruit on a plate in front of him.

"Daddy, what silly thing are you doing now?" Kitsy blurted out when she saw the spectacle.

But the Chief continued to stare until he was sure he had everyone's attention. With a paper napkin he polished the grapefruit carefully and looked at it more intently than ever.

Then in a monotone he began to chant, "I, Abdul Bull-Bull, the seer, have looked into my crystal ball and have solved the mystery of the missing wristwatch."

"Where'd you find it?" Kitsy asked, trying not to show any interest.

"My crystal ball never lies. Here I see various members of the species *Homo sapiens* getting into a station wagon and driving away. They have left behind them a beautiful shiny watch on the table. Now, softly, out of the darkness, creeps *Neotoma cinerea orolestes*. He jumps up on a bench and onto the table. He looks fascinated at the bright object gleaming in the moonlight. Then with his sharp teeth he lifts up the watch by its band, gives three triumphant switches of his long furry tail, jumps down, and retreats into the woods. I, Abdul Bull-Bull, the seer, see that watch resting on a heap of other treasures stolen by *Neotoma cinerea orolestes*. Now the following words come to me— 'Watch, watch out for the watch!' "

"Abdul Corn-Ball!" Buzz said with a grin.

Wiping his brow and coming out of his trance, the Chief looked up in sweet innocence at his audience. "My goodness, I'm hungry!" he said. "When do we eat?"

"You and your stunts! Where is the watch?" Kitsy wanted to know.

"Who's this Neo character?" Phil asked Aunt Amy.

"Oh, Nee-*ott*-o-ma," she pronounced. "That's an ordinary pack rat. They'll steal anything. I wouldn't be surprised if your uncle has a good theory. One thing's sure, if a pack rat took the watch, it won't be far away from camp."

Phil experienced a certain sense of letdown. He had almost convinced himself that the shadowy figure last night had been a thief. Several times in the darkness he had waked and listened for footsteps. And even now he wasn't absolutely convinced that his uncle's knowledge of the ways of animals had solved the mystery of the disappearance of the watch. Nobody had found it yet, and it could be that the Chief was wrong. After all, no rat could have carried off Mr. Post's fishing tackle box. And nobody had yet explained the peculiar behavior of The Dinosaur who certainly seemed to have been "casing the joint."

"Are you going to make us spend all day crawling around looking for a rat's nest?" Buzz asked lazily. "We have to go and see if Three-Toes took his own picture, don't we?"

"*Felis concolor kaibabensis* takes precedence over *Neotoma cinerea orolestes,* or, we'll catch the cat before we catch the rat," the Chief announced with mock importance.

"You and your big words," Kitsy giggled a little scornfully. "When I grow up to be an ologist, I'm going to be the kind that uses language people can understand."

"Then you'd better be a numismatologist," said her father gravely.

"A *what?*"

"That's a guy who studies coins, and money's something everybody can understand."

"Phooey! I'm hungry," Kitsy said. And that ended that.

When the boys and the Chief reached the saddle in the ridge, Phil and Buzz raced toward the catnip scent station, then halted as they came close to the camera and the pie plate that contained the catnip sandwich.

A glance at the camera box showed that the flash bulb had gone off!

"We got him!" Phil shouted triumphantly to his uncle, who hadn't joined in the race.

"Don't disturb anything," the Chief called happily. "I want to get pictures of everything."

He took the camera out of its box and used up the rest of the roll of film, taking photographs of a fresh scratch hill and the scent station, and of the travelway itself.

"Three-Toes might stay around for a few days, with this catnip to sniff and with us to watch," he said. "So we'll reload the camera and set it up again."

This was quickly done.

"Now we're off," the Chief said. The day's work was to consist of following the lion's travelway down into Dry Bones Canyon. If possible, the Chief wanted to map the whole route before the summer was over, in order to see what rhyme or reason there was in the big cat's habits.

The trail was steep, and the farther it went down into the canyon, the steeper it got. Now, instead of walking among fir and spruce trees and aspens that grew in high altitudes, they were passing under tall ponderosa pines which grew lower down. The pines seemed more open and friendly to Phil. He was used to them; there were many of the long-needled trees in the foothills around the out-skirts of his home town. The anxiety that had plagued him all day yesterday had evaporated. He even felt at ease when he looked down a cliff above which the travelway passed.

"We're coming close to the spot that Mr. Post marked on our map," the Chief announced. "If he was right, we ought to be seeing some Kaibab squirrels."

Presently he stopped and pointed at a branch of a pine tree. There a graceful, curling bit of white fluff—the tail of a squirrel—twitched back and forth. At first, it looked like a separate thing and not part of the animal whose dark gray body was almost unnoticeable.

"That's a sight you won't see anywhere else in the world," the Chief said enthusiastically. For once he was so wrapped up in observing an animal that he forgot to do his usual stunt of giving its scientific name.

Now Phil could see the shadowy black underparts of the squirrel, shading into gray on its sides. The little creature darted along the limb, then paused, head down, peering at the human intruders. A big chestnut-colored patch on its back made it seem part of the reddish bark of the pine tree. A moment later it began to scold and stamped one of its feet on the dry stub of a branch that had broken off.

The sight of the little, angry bundle of beauty was so amusing that Phil laughed out loud. Startled, the squirrel fell into momentary silence, then resumed its tirade. Before long another joined in the chorus of protest.

The Chief busied himself with his camera, taking shot after shot of the white-tailed animals who used the spreading branches of the pines as a highway. Happily, Phil and Buzz sat down and watched.

Then the squirrels moved off into other trees and the

"Never mind," Buzz answered.

While Phil was wondering what Buzz had been about to say, the Chief rejoined them, and they decided to eat the sandwiches they had brought in their packsacks. After lunch, they started back up the trail toward the scent station. It was a long, hot climb, but Phil thoroughly enjoyed the workout. When they discovered, at the scent station, that Three-Toes had taken another picture of himself, Phil had a deep sense of satisfaction and pride. He was becoming more and more a part of the expedition, and it was going well.

"We might get still another picture before the old fellow decides to continue on his route," the Chief said. "We'll come back and check again tomorrow." He replaced the flash bulb and turned the film ahead.

"Do you think we'll ever really *see* him?" Phil asked.

"He's around somewhere. But you have to have sharp eyes to see him. He's forty times as big as a house cat, but just as quiet when he walks. A fellow I know was trailed by a lion for a whole day and didn't see it once. He didn't know he'd been trailed until he went back along the same route and found the lion's tracks paralleling his."

Only yesterday Phil had been worried time and again

by the possibility that old Three-Toes might be close by. But today he actually hoped that the big cat was skulking in the woods and that he might catch a glimpse of it. He kept a sharp lookout on both sides of the trail, but now it was curiosity, not fear, that made him study every tree and rock that they passed.

When they reached the point where the trail divided, with the lion's trail going to the left and the old rustlers' path to the right, the Chief stopped a moment. "There's time for one more piece of work," he said. "Let's circle around to that outcrop of rocks behind our tents. I'll give the best hunter an ice-cream soda when we get to Kanab."

"Hunter for what?" Buzz asked.

"For *Neotoma.*"

"For what-oma?" Phil asked.

"You know—the character I saw in my crystal ball this morning. The thief that made off with my watch," the Chief answered.

Phil was astonished. "Are you serious?"

"I think I can afford to buy *one* ice-cream soda—"

"No, I mean do you really think we can find your watch?"

"If I thought it would be hard, I'd offer a reward of

fifty dollars. The watch is worth a hundred. So you can judge for yourself."

Phil looked at his uncle and had a feeling that for once he wasn't kidding.

"Look in every protected spot under overhanging rocks where a rat could build a nest and keep dry. If you see a big bundle of stuff that seems all woven together, that's probably *Neotoma's* house. And somewhere near, is likely to be his treasure pile. Let's go."

Small ledges of grayish limestone thrust up out of the hillside all along here. The boys began looking at the bottom of each outcrop and in every crack in the weathered rock surfaces.

They were getting tired, when the Chief called, "Hey, it's past quitting time. Five minutes after five. Let's knock off and go home."

"How do you know what time it is?" Buzz asked.

His father ostentatiously pointed to his wrist. And there was the missing watch!

"Where did you find it?" Phil cried.

"Right here. I'm going to take a picture of this miser's hoard." There, in a cranny under a big rock, was just the kind of nest the Chief had told the boys to look for. "He must have had a good time while the construction men were fixing our campsite up."

In a neat pile near the nest lay shiny, chewing-gum wrappers, cigarette packages, a spoon—and a silver dollar.

"Hey, there's my dollar!" Buzz shouted.

Phil looked at him suspiciously. "How much money *do* you have?" he asked.

"I told you I had two dollars—" Buzz reached down and picked up the coin "—and now I've still got two dollars."

"You didn't say you lost any," Phil remarked.

"Oh, I almost told you when we were resting down in Dry Bones Canyon. But I figured it might turn up."

The Chief was mildly interested in the conversation, but didn't say anything until he had taken the picture. Then he announced, "All right, I'll collect that ice-cream soda from you on Monday, Buzz."

"Hey, you promised *us* a soda if we found your watch. We didn't promise you anything!" Buzz protested.

"Cheapskates!" his father snorted cheerfully, and strode into camp brandishing his arm so that his wife and Kitsy could see the watch.

11　　　　　　　　　　**A TRAP IS SET**

"Thank goodness it's *you!*" Aunt Amy exclaimed as the boys and the Chief came into camp. "You don't know what a fright you gave me, rustling around in the brush! I didn't think you'd come home from that direction."

Phil was very much surprised. This didn't sound at all like his usually calm and placid aunt. The Chief, too, sensed something very unusual in his wife's excitement.

"What's the matter, Amy?" he asked.

"Somebody was here today, while Kitsy and I were out bird-watching," she answered. "They were just tearing down the boys' tent when I surprised them—or him, I don't know which. Whoever it was ran away into the woods, right where you came from!"

"You must be imagining things, Amy. It was probably Lulubelle up to more tricks."

"Lulubelle might have knocked the tent over, but she doesn't leave footprints like that—"

Phil and Buzz whirled around and saw that one side of their tent was collapsed and sagging sloppily inward. Three stakes had been uprooted, and the wall of the tent had pulled away from the trench. There in the disturbed earth were two large prints made by boots or shoes.

"I heard them—or him—running away, up through the woods, Herbert. I certainly was not imagining things."

Phil could see easily enough that the prints had not been made by anyone in their party. The boots were bigger than his or Buzz's or the Chief's.

"Last night your watch disappeared, Herbert. And today when we were all gone, somebody came and tried some more monkey business. I've been looking around to see if anything else has been stolen."

"Now, Amy, you're getting jumpy. See, we found the watch just where I thought we would, in a rat's nest."

Aunt Amy looked confused. Phil stared at his aunt and uncle. For once their roles seemed to be switched. The Chief was being the calm one and Aunt Amy appeared all flustered and excited.

"So we found the watch," Buzz said seriously, "but I

think a lot of things need explaining, Chief. The Dinosaur, for instance; Mr. Post's missing tackle box; and now this tent business. There would be hoofprints here if Lulubelle or some other deer had pushed our tent over."

"All right, Sherlock," the Chief said with a grin. "Here *are* some hoofprints." He pointed to undeniable deep marks in the soil along the trench.

"Yes," Buzz admitted, "but who was in the shoes that left these footprints? The toes are *under* the place where the floor of the tent was."

"You've got something there," his father agreed. But he went on, "I have an idea what happened. Some smart-alecky tourist saw the 'Private' sign on our road. He figured if there was some place he shouldn't go, that was exactly where he wanted to go. He came down here and had some kind of argument with Lulubelle. She got tangled up in the tent—that's why her footprints are there—and the tourist came over to see what damage had been done. But at that moment Amy appeared. So the tourist got worried about being caught inside a 'Private' sign, and he beat it, as fast as he could go."

"You may be right, Herbert," said Aunt Amy. "But I'm perfectly sure it wasn't a deer I heard running."

Kitsy, who had been silently hugging the lion kitten, spoke up in a thin, frightened voice. "It wasn't a deer."

The Chief sat down next to Kitsy on the camp bench and put his arm around her. "It's all right, honey. We have it all figured out. Now don't you worry. On Monday we're going to Kanab, and you can take Oliver with you. You haven't even heard what the boys and I did today."

"That's right," Aunt Amy said. "How did your trip go? I was so upset I forgot to ask you."

The Chief patted his pocket. "I have a picture of Three-Toes right here. And there's another one in the camera. I hope to have still another by tomorrow morning. Next week I'll develop them. Boyd Blake has a darkroom."

"Kitsy and I got some good pictures of a dusky grouse and her eight little ones—didn't we? You can develop them at the same time," Aunt Amy said in a voice that Phil knew she tried to make reassuring for Kitsy's benefit.

"Come on," Phil said to Buzz. "We better fix our tent."

As the two boys drove the tent stakes back into the ground, the Chief bustled around. "Mrs. Fletcher," he said importantly, "there are five hungry naturalists here. What do you think we can do about the situation?"

"Six. You forgot Oliver," Kitsy said. "I have to make

his formula and warm his bottle."

The camp had all the outward appearances of returning to normal, but Phil and Buzz weren't satisfied. And it seemed to Phil that at least Aunt Amy wasn't convinced that Lulubelle was the culprit who bashed in their tent.

It was a somewhat subdued group that sat around the campfire that night. Everyone seemed glad to have his own private thoughts interrupted when Boyd Blake arrived unannounced.

"You folks look mighty comfortable," the Ranger said. "May I join you? Did you get a picture of Three-Toes?"

"We certainly did," Buzz answered.

Coming quickly to the point of his visit, Blake said, "Chief, I have a favor to ask of you. A professor arrived in the Park today with a bunch of kids in one of those traveling summer schools. The professor knows about you and wanted to meet you right away and ask you to lecture to his students. I told him you'd left word not to be bothered by anybody, but I promised I'd deliver his invitation. He'd like it if you'd give a little talk on wildlife tomorrow."

"Nothing doing," the Chief said politely. "We've had too many interruptions. I need to get some work done."

"Unfortunately," Boyd Blake went on, as if he hadn't

heard, "I told him you had made a wonderful recording of a mountain lion's scream—"

"*He* made!" Buzz protested. "Phil and I made it."

"Blake," the Chief said with a twinkle in his eye, "those boys were sound asleep when that recording was made. —All right, tell the fellow I'll talk to his students."

Phil was perfectly certain that the Chief had suddenly realized the possibilities of making a wonderful yarn out of the lion's scream.

"That's fine," the Ranger said. "I'll do something for you sometime."

"You can begin by letting me use your darkroom to develop some pictures before the lecture," the Chief told him. "And then you can do something about an old-maid doe that hangs around here causing trouble. Today she bashed in the boy's tent."

"Yeah, I heard about her," Boyd Blake said quickly. "The fellow who picked up garbage here today was talking about what a nuisance she is. He said she'd made a real mess of your camp. Tell you what—you people just get tough with her and keep chasing her away. I think she'll lose interest in your camp. But if she does cause you any more trouble, I'll have her picked up and moved away."

After the Ranger left, the Chief said, "Well, that's a relief. We know now that we don't have to worry about the owner of those footprints."

"Don't be silly, Daddy," said Kitsy. "The garbage truck wasn't here when Mommy and I came back and found the tent pushed in. And anyway, why would the garbage man run away up the hill?"

"Kitsy, that was Lulubelle who made a racket going up that hill. Let's not talk about it anymore. We're all getting the jitters, and there's nothing to be jittery about. Tell me something—why did the little moron decide to walk home instead of taking the bus?"

"I don't know," Kitsy answered dully.

"Because she—" Phil began.

"The little moron isn't a she," Kitsy said with more life. "He's a he. Always. Well, why didn't he take the bus?"

"He was afraid his mother would make him take it back."

"Oh, you!" Kitsy said, and comforted she went off to bed.

The next morning, while the Chief made notes for his lecture, Phil and Buzz walked up to the scent station to see if Three-Toes had taken another picture of himself. The flash bulb had not gone off. This meant that the lion had not been around. And so, as the Chief had told them to do, the boys dismantled the photographic trap.

Phil had made up his mind that he was going to stay around camp as long as the Chief was away. He felt pretty sure that nothing would happen to frighten Kitsy and Aunt Amy if he and Buzz were there. Buzz apparently felt the same way. Although neither of them said a word of his private thoughts, they both managed to find ways of spending the day close to the tents.

Altogether it was a boring day, and Phil was glad when the Chief returned at last, with a beautiful photograph of Three-Toes that he had developed and a hilarious report on his lecture.

In the tent that night, Phil whispered to Buzz, "You know, I think somebody besides Lulubelle and the garbage collector was messing around here yesterday."

"I've been thinking the same thing," Buzz agreed. "I'll bet anything it was The Dinosaur. Maybe he's crazy. You have to admit The Dinosaur is a funny-*looking* guy."

"Another thing," Phil went on. "If we're all away from here, all day tomorrow in Kanab—and if it is The Dinosaur or somebody like that—he'll be sure to come again while we're gone. Maybe we ought to stay here on guard."

"Are you crazy yourself?" Buzz asked. "We have to go

to Kanab and buy our Geiger counter."

"Well—what'll we do?"

There was a long silence. Then, "I've got it!" Phil whispered. "We'll set up the camera trap, somehow, when the Chief isn't looking. Then, if The Dinosaur comes snooping around, we'll have a picture of him."

"Man, oh, man, you've got a real idea!" Buzz said joyfully. "But what can we use for bait, so as to be sure he'll step on the switch?"

For a long time the two of them lay in silence, puzzling. Then Phil began to think out loud. "Lions like catnip sandwiches. People like sandwiches, but that wouldn't do. The Dinosaur would suspect a trap if we left anything to eat. Anyway, Lulubelle or the rat would steal it."

"Maybe we could leave something valuable that a thief would want to steal," Buzz suggested.

"Who wants to have anything stolen?"

"Yeah, I know. I'm just trying to have an idea."

"Eureka!" Phil said in a loud voice.

"Hey, shut up!" Buzz cautioned him. "We're supposed to be asleep."

"I've got it!" Phil whispered. "Anybody who hangs around spying on us is bound to get thirsty. Sooner or later he'll want a drink out of our water faucet. If we put the switch down underneath the board by the faucet where he's *got* to step when he turns on the water—it's simple. The faucet is our bait!"

"Einstein, you're right!" Buzz said enthusiastically. "We'll clamp the camera to the fir tree. And we won't need a flash bulb, because the faucet is right out in the sun all day long. He'll never know he's taken his own picture."

The boys completed their plans, and finally dropped off to sleep. The most important element of their scheme was Kitsy. They had to get her co-operation. Next morning, Phil drew her aside and explained their plan to catch the man who had knocked over their tent. They didn't want to tell the grownups, because it was going to be a surprise. After breakfast Kitsy must wander off to the far end of the meadow. There she would put Oliver up into the crotch of an aspen tree. Next, she must yell and insist that *both* of her *parents* come and help get the lion kitten down. While they were rescuing Oliver, the boys would set up the camera trap for the prowler.

Delighted with the idea, Kitsy agreed.

Things went according to schedule. Phil dug out a hole for the camera switch under the plank beside the water faucet. Buzz cut away a couple of branches on the fir tree, to make a place where the camera could be clamped.

Working feverishly, the two boys fixed the camera in place, laid the wire and kicked some twigs and dirt over it to make it unobtrusive, and rigged the connections to by-pass the flash-bulb attachment. They had barely finished when Oliver and his rescuers returned.

Kitsy's role had been the hardest in the plot. Once in the tree, Oliver had taken to climbing. With her father's help, Kitsy had had to scramble up after him.

"It was scary up there," she reported. Then she whispered to Phil, "Is it all fixed?"

"Sh! It's okay."

"It better be. I got a good scolding on account of you."

"Don't you worry. It'll be worth it," Buzz promised her.

On the long drive into Kanab, Phil almost wished he could have stayed in camp to see what happened. But, as the station wagon went down and down the northern slopes of the Kaibab Plateau toward the low, hot valley and the old Mormon town of Kanab, his thoughts began to turn to the Geiger counter and the twenty dollars in his wallet. This was a secret he was *not* going to tell Kitsy. At least not until after he and Buzz had found uranium.

12   THE DINOSAUR AGAIN

Phil's eyes were fascinated with the sight of a town again. Kanab, moreover, was not like any town he had ever seen. There were old brick buildings built long ago by Mormon settlers, sleek modern filling stations, Navaho women in long, bright satin skirts who carried babies strapped to cradle boards. Here was a place to spend a whole day just looking.

The Chief parked in the shade of a big cottonwood tree, so that the station wagon wouldn't be too hot a cage in which to leave Oliver. Kitsy was undecided. She wanted to see the town, and she also wanted to stay with her pet. But Oliver had been so quiet riding along that she decided it was all right to leave him for a while.

"I'll expect to collect that ice-cream soda, boys, just as soon as Amy and I get through buying food at the supermarket," said the Chief. "I'll meet you right here in half an hour."

"Just try and collect!" Phil said with a grin.

"Ice cream spoils your appetite," Buzz added. Then he asked, "Ma, do we have to take Kitsy with us?"

"No, she's coming with me. I have to buy her some new sneakers," his mother answered.

With triumphant sighs of relief, Phil and Buzz watched until Kitsy and her parents had disappeared into the market. Then they hurried along the street, looking into stores until they came to one that had a large display of minerals in the front window and a sign that said: GEIGER COUNTERS.

Inside they found shelves and showcases containing everything a uranium prospector might need: geologist's hammers, canteens, sleeping bags, tarpaulins, Army surplus goods. And Geiger counters in all sizes and shapes.

"We want to buy a Geiger counter," Phil said to the man who stood leaning against a big pile of blankets. "We don't care if it's secondhand, as long as it works."

The man didn't move. "Over there in that case, I've got a dandy that's worth five hundred dollars new. I'll let you have it for half price."

"Oh, we don't mean an expensive one like that," Phil

said quickly. "Haven't you got something cheaper?"

"Sure. I have all kinds. Where are you prospecting?"

Phil and Buzz were both embarrassed and cautious. "Oh, around—places. We just want to try."

"How much money have you got to spend?"

"Twenty-two dollars," Phil blurted out.

The storekeeper seemed to feel he had something solid to work with now, and he opened up the showcase. He took out a small Geiger counter, badly scratched on the outside. "This is a dandy. I can let you have it for twenty-five."

"How do we know if it works?" Buzz asked doubtfully.

"How do you know if it works! Want to try it out?" The storekeeper set the machine on top of the showcase. "Put these on," he said, handing Buzz a set of earphones. Then he turned a switch. "Hear anything?"

Buzz nodded. "It goes click-click-click."

"That's what we call the background count. It doesn't mean anything, except that the machine is working. Now wait a minute." The storekeeper went to the front window, picked up a chunk of yellow ore, and brought it back. The minute he held it close to the counter, Buzz's face lit up.

"Wow! It's gone crazy!" Buzz shouted.

"Let me listen," Phil demanded. He reached out to take

the earphones. Buzz shied away from him.

Phil shouted, hoping Buzz would hear in spite of the earphones, "Whose twenty dollars is it?"

"Twenty dollars!" said the storekeeper. "I thought you said twenty-two. And anyway, it costs twenty-five."

"I'm putting up twenty, and he's got two," Phil explained.

"I get it," the man said. He reached for the earphones and turned them over to Phil.

To demonstrate the wonders of the machine, he took the piece of ore away, then once again moved it gradually toward the Geiger counter. As the ore approached, Phil heard the clicks of the counter increase in frequency until there was a constant hum in his ears. Finally the man put the ore specimen in the window again and came back.

"It's a good little machine," he said. "But you have to take care of it. The batteries are new, but be careful not to waste them. Always turn off the switch when you aren't using it. Don't leave it out in the rain so it gets wet."

Phil looked at Buzz, and Buzz stared back. What could they do? They had only twenty-two dollars and a little change. The one thing Phil could think of was to take out his money and show it. He opened his wallet and laid four five-dollar bills on top of a table. From his pocket he fished a quarter, a dime, and three cents. Buzz planked down his two silver dollars. He had two dimes in addition.

"Twenty-two fifty-eight," Phil said. "That's all we've got. No fooling. And we *have* to have a Geiger counter."

"I'll tell you, fellows," the storekeeper said. "It's been a slow day, and you can have it. But if you strike it rich, bring me the difference."

"Gee, thanks!" Phil said and grabbed the little machine. "Could you wrap it up? We've got reasons."

"You're just like the rest of the prospectors that come in here." The storekeeper grinned. "Everybody's trying to keep his uranium a secret from everybody else." But he did fish out a crumpled bag from under a pile of merchandise and Phil thrust the machine into it.

"Wait a minute!" the man called as the boys started for the door. "I thought I told you to turn that thing off when you weren't using it. You'll use up the battery."

Phil looked inside the bag. The man was right. The switch was still on. "Boy, we got to be careful," he said to Buzz. "Thanks, mister. See you later."

Out on the street, Buzz said to Phil, "The folks aren't in sight. That's good. I'll run into the supermarket and get the station wagon key and tell 'em we'll wait and keep Oliver happy. We can stash the package under the blanket in the back and they'll never know the difference."

Phil waited nervously at some distance from the station wagon. A group of small boys had gathered and were staring through the side window at the oversized spotted kitten. When Buzz ran up with the key, one of the boys asked, "Doesn't he bite?"

"No. Get out of the way now, please," Buzz replied.

Cautiously he opened the door and caught the kitten as it tried to wedge its way out. Phil climbed in behind him, and a minute later they had the Geiger counter hidden under an old blanket on the floor behind the front seat.

When the large bundles of groceries arrived, they were stowed in the rear, while Kitsy came and took charge of Oliver. By now the kitten was excited, for the curious youngsters had been scratching on the windows and making loud noises at him.

"If you're going to see Mr. Post with us, Kitsy, you'll have to bring Oliver along," the Chief said. "Snap his leash on his collar, so he can't get away."

Phil looked up quickly at Buzz. In their excitement over the Geiger counter, the two of them had forgotten that they planned to visit Mr. Post.

"Well, hello!" The jeweler looked surprised to see them. Then he smiled jovially as they trooped in with a procession of small boys following Kitsy—or rather, following Oliver who perched on her shoulder. "I didn't expect to see you in Kanab quite so soon." He reached over the counter to shake hands with the Chief.

"These two boys had bigger appetites than we realized," the Chief answered. "We ran out of food ahead of schedule. Besides, we were getting hungry for some fresh meat. You can't buy it in the Park, as I guess you know."

"I wish I'd have thought about that," Mr. Post said. "I could have brought you anything you wanted when I was up there fishing on the weekend."

"Did you catch any?" Buzz asked.

"No, I didn't have much luck. They weren't biting. If they had been, I'd sure have brought you a mess of trout. I went down Bright Angel Creek, but I'd have done better if I'd tried my old stamping grounds in Dry Bones Canyon."

"You've given me an idea, Mr. Post," the Chief said. "When will you be fishing in the Park again? The reason I ask is this: It *would* be a great help if you'd bring us some meat and green vegetables when you come."

"Why, I'm bringing Mrs. Post up on Thursday. We're

going to have a long weekend in the Park. I suppose you wouldn't need anything that soon."

"Oh, yes, indeed I will," Aunt Amy said. "I'll just plan my menus differently. It would be wonderful if you could bring us some beeksteak and lettuce and fresh fruit."

"If you're sure you don't mind," the Chief said, pulling out his wallet. "I'll leave you money to pay for the groceries right now."

"It's a deal," Mr. Post said.

While the talk about groceries went on, Phil was growing more and more impatient. At last he was able to break in. "Say, Mr. Post, did they ever catch the burglar who stole your stuff?"

"Not yet," the jeweler said, with a serious look on his face. "But the police say they're still working on it." He came out from behind the glass case that held a small display of watches, rings, and bracelets in velvet-lined boxes and walked over to the door. "Whoever did it cut a hole in the door around the lock. He used a brace and bit to do it. All the valuable stuff I had was in the safe. The fellow must have been a real professional. He worked the combination on the safe and didn't use TNT or tools of any kind."

"Man, oh man!" Phil exclaimed. He had seen plenty

of movies and read plenty of stories, but he had never been on the scene where a real crime had taken place.

"One thing I've never been able to understand," the Chief said. "Why would a man, who has the intelligence and skill to feel out a combination with his fingers, go into a risky line of work like safe-cracking? Most of them seem to get caught sooner or later—the business doesn't pay."

"It takes all kinds to make the world, I guess," Mr. Post answered. "Anyway, live and learn, I always say. I've got a burglar alarm rigged up that's supposed to be foolproof now. . . . But what about you folks? Having a good time? How's your expedition going? I see you've collected a specimen already." He nodded toward Oliver.

The lion kitten had quieted down, now that the small boys had grown bored and had gone back into the street.

"Isn't a cat like that dangerous to have around?" Mr. Post asked.

"Oh, Kitsy has him tamed," the Chief said a little proudly.

"Are you going to take him down to Phantom Ranch with you, sister?" Mr. Post asked. "You'll have to teach him to ride on a mule, if you want to do that."

"Kitsy could probably teach him even that," the Chief

said. "But the Rangers will take care of him while we're gone." Then he snapped his fingers, the way he did when he recalled something he should have thought of before. "Remind me, Amy. I must warn Boyd Blake that he'll have to give Oliver room and board starting the sixteenth or seventeenth."

"Perhaps you don't know it," Mr. Post said, "but there is limited space at Phantom Ranch. You have to make reservations or else you won't have a place to stay."

"That's right," the Chief said. Then he turned to the others. "I seem to remember that somebody promised somebody an ice-cream soda."

"See you on Thursday," Mr. Post called after them as they left the store.

Outside, the boys glanced around in search of an ice-cream parlor sign. Phil looked directly across the street, and there, in a window, he saw something that startled him. He grabbed Buzz by the arm.

"Look over there," he said. "Do you see what I see in that restaurant?"

The head of a man showed above the low curtain in the restaurant window.

Staring out at them was The Dinosaur!

13

"Chief!" Buzz said quietly, walking up close to his father. "There's that guy spying on us again."

"What are you talking about? Who's spying?"

"You know—the one we call The Dinosaur."

"You're imagining things, Buzz. Why would anybody spy on us?"

"But we saw him! He was staring at us right out of that window back there. Ask Phil," Buzz said earnestly.

Phil came up on the other side of his uncle. "No fooling, Chief, we saw that Dinosaur again, and he was watching everything we did. Remember how we caught him spying on our camp?"

"I'll bet he's the one that knocked the tent over before Mom frightened him away," Buzz added.

"Come down to earth, you two!" the Chief laughed.

"You're just dizzy with hunger. Here's a drugstore. Let's get some food into you."

"What are you men plotting?" Aunt Amy asked.

"Nothing important," her husband answered. "Let's take on some calories and head for home."

Phil nudged Buzz and shook his head sadly. Their camera trap would be a big fizzle. The Dinosaur was here in Kanab so they couldn't get a picture of him while he prowled around their camp. Moreover, the Chief was sure to kid the daylights out of them when he found out they had rigged a trap to catch a prowler who wasn't there.

Both boys kept silent most of the way home as the station wagon pulled steadily up from the low, hot country around Kanab into the high cool forest on top of the plateau. Before they drew into camp, they had quietly worked out a plan to solve their complicated problem. They had to get their Geiger counter into their tent before anybody saw it; and they wanted to dismantle the camera trap, if possible, without being noticed. Buzz was to take charge of the counter. After he had stowed it in the tent, he was to divert the attention of the others while Phil recovered the camera.

Things started to work out pretty well. Phil helped his aunt and uncle lug bundles and groceries over to the camp table. Kitsy, fortunately, had to fix a bottle for Oliver. This gave Buzz a chance to sneak his package into the boys' tent and hide it under his sleeping bag. Then he came out and stumbled dramatically.

"Oh, my toe, my toe!" he yelled.

His mother, father, and sister all came running.

"What's the matter?" the Chief asked.

But before Buzz could even answer, Phil shouted, "Hey! We got the picture!"

The injured toe healed in a flash, and Buzz ran toward the fir tree where the camera had been fastened inconspicuously. No question about it; the little electromagnet had tripped the shutter. Somebody had stepped on the board. There was a picture of him on the roll of film!

"We caught the prowler!" Phil shouted gleefully.

When explanations had been made, the Chief thought for a moment. Then he announced: "I'm going to put a stop to these silly notions about dinosaurs and prowlers. We'll go right up to Boyd Blake's house and develop this film. Even though I do have to waste the rest of the roll. Obviously Lulubelle stepped on your board, but I have to prove it to you. And after that I want it understood that no one is to tamper with this camera without permission. It's quite possible that you boys have spoiled my second lion picture. And I want no more talk about prowlers and such. We came out here on a scientific expedition, and you are trying to make it seem like a movie mystery."

The boys edged away toward their tent. "Your dad seems really sore at us, Buzz," Phil said. "I don't see why."

"He'll find out what we're talking about when the picture is developed," Buzz fumed. "He'll have to admit we aren't such nuts as he thinks we are. There *is* something fishy going on, but he won't believe it till we prove it to him."

"Then maybe he'll calm down," Phil said doubtfully.

"Maybe he'll just get more excited in a different direction. Maybe he'll say we have to move our camp, and that'll just mean work for us," Buzz said in a glum voice.

Without waiting for supper, the Chief hustled the boys into the station wagon and headed for the cabin near headquarters where Boyd Blake and his wife lived. The Ranger wasn't at home, but Mrs. Blake, who was a hospitable young woman, told the Chief he was welcome to use the little darkroom she and her husband had improvised in a shed attached to the cabin. Phil and Buzz sat on the steps.

There would be a tedious wait. The boys were finally reduced to playing ticktacktoe, scratching lines with sticks on the gravel path. Buzz had piled up an impressive series of victories when Boyd Blake arrived in his truck.

"Hello! Do you know you fellows are famous? Ever since the Chief gave his lecture yesterday, the kids who heard him talk have been trying to find out where you're camped, so they can meet the boys who recorded the lion's snore and the scientist's scream."

"Send 'em around. We charge a quarter for our autographs," Buzz said. "And we happen to be broke."

"Big sale—two autographs for forty-nine cents," Phil added. "Bring on those kids!"

"I'm afraid you'll have to get your money the hard way," Blake said with a grin. "I promised the Chief I wouldn't reveal his hideaway. Where is he, anyway?"

Just then the Chief emerged from the darkroom. Obviously he was both excited and at a loss for words. "Boyd," he said, "I wish you'd come and have a look."

"We did get a picture of the prowler!" Phil muttered to Buzz. "Look at the way your dad's acting."

"Chief! Let us look!" Their eagerness to see what was on the film was like an intense physical pain.

The Chief paid no attention. He kept on talking in a low voice to Boyd Blake.

Then suddenly there came a hoot of laughter. First it was only Boyd Blake, then the Chief joined in.

"Go and look, boys," the Ranger said, coming out of the door, his face smiling and still flushed with laughter.

"What's so funny?" Buzz snapped.

A sudden feeling of uncertainty and embarrassment came over Phil. It seemed plain that he and Buzz were being laughed at, although he couldn't see why.

"Be sure and make some extra prints for me," Boyd Blake called back, as he went into his cabin for dinner.

Gingerly Phil stepped into the darkroom and peered through the gadget that enlarged the film. There was the water faucet—and there was the rear view of a man leaning over to take a drink. All Phil could see clearly was the seat of the man's pants.

"Well, there's the prowler," the Chief chuckled.

Buzz elbowed Phil out of the way and took a look. "What's so funny?" he said. "It *is* somebody that sneaked up when we were gone."

"It's an arch prowler, a snooper par excellence. Future generations will look with awe on this self-taken portrait of the south end of an outlaw going north. The criminal, my fine detectives, is none other than Boyd Blake!"

14

On the way back to camp, Phil and Buzz sat in silent mortification. It didn't help when the Chief broke out a couple of times in a chuckle. The boys' plan had fizzled because The Dinosaur was in Kanab, and that was bad enough. But it was almost more than they could bear to be laughed at for photographing the seat of Boyd Blake's pants.

At last the Chief became more serious, and even a little sympathetic. "I have to give you fellows credit for thinking up a really smart idea," he said. "If there *had* been a prowler, you would certainly have caught him. And the whole thing has helped to clear the air."

Phil grunted and Buzz shrugged.

"You know what has been the matter with all of us?" the Chief went on. "The altitude has been affecting us. It does that, you know. People who come up into high country very often get nervous and jittery, and it takes them a while to calm down. When we arrived, we were already tired from the year of schoolwork and making a long, fast trip to get here. Our nerves were on edge, and we began to imagine things. From now on we'll be all right."

It was a relief, Phil thought, that the Chief wasn't poking fun at them any more. But it was a letdown to find that their detective work had ended in a joke. And he wasn't at all convinced by the Chief's lecture on jitters. Too many things remained unexplained. For instance, Mr. Post's missing tackle box. Or was it still missing? They hadn't asked. Anyway, jitters didn't explain The Dinosaur's spying.

A good, hot dinner helped to take away Phil's sense of disappointment. In the end, he and Buzz helped tell the story to Kitsy and Aunt Amy.

"Now that things have calmed down," the Chief said as they sat around the campfire, "let's talk about our next project. Old Three-Toes has undoubtedly moved on and won't be back for three weeks. So we'll hunt bats."

Phil listened with only half an ear. He was wondering how he could get a chance to use the Geiger counter, and he suspected, from the vacant stare on Buzz's face, that his cousin was thinking about the same thing. The worst of it was that the Chief's plans for the next few days seemed to fill up every hour. When would they get a chance to go out prospecting for uranium?

"The experts all believe," the Chief was saying, "that there must be at least four species of bats that live here on the North Rim that nobody has ever found yet."

"How do they know if they haven't seen them?" Kitsy demanded.

"Well, these bats live in other places at the same altitude and in the same climate. It's just a good guess that they must be here, too. I want to find them if I can, and then we'll do some experimenting."

The mention of experiments roused some interest in Phil. "What can you do to bats that proves anything?" he asked.

"First of all, there's a great mystery about where certain bats spend a lot of their time. Nobody knows where the males go while the females are rearing the young, for example. And nobody knows yet what the real explanation is for the homing instinct of bats."

"You mean like homing pigeons?" Kitsy asked.

"It seems to be about the same thing," her father replied. "But scientists aren't sure. They do know how bats can fly in the dark without bumping into things. But how they can keep their sense of direction is something else again."

"But does anybody really know they come home like pigeons?" Phil asked in disbelief.

"Scientists catch them and put bands on them for identification. Then they carry a whole load of them miles away and let them loose. And the bats turn up at their roosts later on. When we catch some, we'll do the same."

By now Phil's interest was really roused. It would be all right to go bat hunting if they could just find some way to discover uranium at the same time without getting into trouble with the Chief.

"Well, if we're going to make an early start tomorrow, we'd better go to bed," Aunt Amy said, speaking for the first time in the whole evening.

"Okay, bed it is," the Chief agreed. He shoveled earth onto the fire to make sure it couldn't flare up during the night and start a forest fire. Kitsy, the baby lion in her arms, overtook the boys heading for their tent.

"That wasn't a deer Mommy and I heard when we came back to camp that day," she said quietly.

"How do you know?" Phil asked.

"Anybody knows how a deer sounds," she answered.

"What do you want us to do about it?" Buzz asked her.

"I don't know. I'm just telling you."

"Maybe you're imagining things," Buzz said.

"Oh, don't talk like Mommy!" Kitsy answered.

Phil was interested in what she said, but he had more immediate things on his mind.

"It looks like we'll have to use our Geiger counter at night," he said to Buzz when they got inside the tent. "Let's start tonight. We can go as soon as your folks are asleep."

"It's a deal!" Buzz whispered.

As quietly as they could, they unwrapped the Geiger counter. The rustling paper seemed to make an infernal racket, but apparently it wasn't heard in the adjoining tent. Presently all was silence there, and then the rhythmic rumble of the Chief's snores gave proof that he was asleep.

Stealthily the two boys stepped out and skirted the camp, walking on the soft meadow grass. When they thought they were a safe distance away, they turned up the hill that lay below Rustlers' Fort.

By the time they had reached the first outcropping of rock, they were far enough away to feel safe in talking.

"Choose you for it," Phil said. "Odds or evens—winner gets first listen."

Solemnly they faced each other in a strip of moonlight and each thrust his right hand toward the other. "One—two—three—"

Buzz won. Quickly he fitted on the earphones and turned the switch.

"There's the clicking we heard in the store. What did he call it? Background count?"

He held the counter close to a big rock and moved it all around. "Nothing here," he reported. Still wearing the earphones, he moved through the underbrush toward another outcrop.

"Hey, turn it off when you're not listening." Phil raised his voice. Apparently Buzz couldn't hear because of the earphones. Phil stepped up and tugged at his jacket. Then he reached down and turned the switch.

"What do you want to do that for?" Buzz demanded. "I'm listening."

"That man told us to save the batteries. You're only supposed to use the counter when you see a bunch of rocks. A lot of dirt over the rocks stops the radiations."

"Well, maybe there isn't a *lot* of dirt here."

"Maybe there is."

"Oh, all right."

Buzz tried a second outcrop but had no luck.

"My turn now," Phil said. "I'll take the next two rocks."

"Don't be in such a hurry. I just got started."

"Oh, come *on!*" Phil forgot caution, and his voice rose.

"Come on is right!" another voice called from farther down the hill. "What are you boys up to?"

The beam of a flashlight stabbed in their direction.

"Now you've done it!" Buzz said. "The Chief heard you, and he's right down there."

"I couldn't help it!" Phil answered defensively. "Quick, we got to hide the counter."

Thinking fast, Phil peeled off his jacket, wrapped the machine in it, and poked it between two rocks.

"What in the name of common sense are you two idiots doing up here?" the Chief demanded. "Scaring the daylights out of us when you're supposed to be asleep."

"How did you know we were out?" Buzz asked. "We didn't make any noise."

"Kitsy heard your footsteps and was frightened. She woke me. *What are you up to?*"

"Nothing," Phil answered. "We weren't sleepy and the moonlight was so nice we decided to take a walk."

His uncle glanced at him. "Where's your jacket, young

man? You'll catch pneumonia."

"I—I guess I must have dropped it when you yelled and scared us," Phil answered. "I had it. I'm not that dumb. I'll go back and get it."

"No, you will not! You're going to bed now. You'll get it in the morning. And both of you will get a few more well-chosen words. Good *night!*"

"Whew-ee!" Phil whispered to Buzz after they had crawled into their sleeping bags. "That was a close one."

Next morning Phil managed to recover his jacket and smuggle the Geiger counter into the tent without being noticed. The Chief had forgotten his grudge and was intent on the day's bat-hunting trip. Aunt Amy had been up since before dawn getting some early-morning bird calls on the tape recorder, and she was so delighted with the songs she had heard that she scarcely remembered to lecture the boys for the fright they had given her the night before. Only Kitsy pursued the subject.

"I think you're mean to scare us," she said. "You sounded just like whoever it was that Mommy and I heard the day your tent was pushed over."

"Oh, snap out of it," Buzz answered. "How many times do you have to be told that that was probably Lulubelle?"

For the next three days, Phil and Buzz had no time to use their Geiger counter, but life was full of the kind of excitement they had looked forward to when they set out on the expedition.

Their first bat trip took them to the rim of the Canyon, then down over it through a break in the sheer cliff wall. The route went straight down an almost perpendicular gash in the rock. Phil enjoyed every tense moment of struggle in the mountaineering problem the three of them had to solve, just as he enjoyed a tough game on the basketball court. Here was an opponent to be licked. Using handholds and footholds in the rock, while empty space yawned below him on one side, he conquered the descent.

At the bottom of this chute was a ledge along which they could walk for some distance. It was perfectly solid, but time and again Phil found himself rubbing his left shoulder as close as possible to the rock wall to keep away from the yawning depth at his right. Then the ledge widened, and he dared to think of something besides his immediate safety.

"Clickety-clickety!" he muttered to Buzz, nodding toward a band of red sandstone below them.

Buzz put his hands over his ears and grinned. He got the point about the Geiger counter.

They rounded a corner, and a new stretch of the red rocks appeared.

"Clickety-clickety!" Buzz called.

"Click-click-click!" Phil came back. Then he realized that the Chief was staring at them in wonder.

A little way ahead, a dark hole appeared in the limestone wall at their left. All of a sudden the Chief pointed, then whirled around toward them. "Clickety-clickety-click!" he said solemnly.

The two boys almost fell off the ledge in laughter. Then Buzz managed to splutter out, "Clickety-click."

The brilliant sun beat down on them, but a cool breeze blew out of the cave entrance when they reached it.

"Lunch time," the Chief announced. "After that we'll

take a look inside. Blake says it's safe to walk into it, and it doesn't go back very far."

In the shade offered by the cave, which arched a couple of feet higher than their heads, they ate their lunch.

"Boy, I've never been so thirsty!" Phil commented.

"If you think you're thirsty now," his uncle said, "just wait till we make our trip to Phantom Ranch. On the way back out of the Canyon you'll think you're in the middle of the Sahara Desert. There's only one place to get a drink in the last five miles."

From the mouth of the cave, the boys looked down, probing without success for the little glint that would be the Colorado River at the bottom of the canyon. In a couple of weeks, if the Fletcher party kept to its schedule, they would take the long trip on muleback down the Kaibab Trail to the place where the clear water of Bright Angel Creek joined the muddy torrent of the great, gnawing river.

But right now they had bats to look for in the cool cave. As far as they could see into the darkness the walls were bare and smooth. Turning on his flashlight, the Chief led the way. After about fifty feet or so, the tunnel took a sharp bend, and they found themselves in utter blackness. No rays of sunshine could penetrate here.

"There they are!" the Chief exclaimed. "Look at 'em." His flashlight beam played along the ceiling of the tunnel. Phil made out odd-shaped, dark masses at several points. They were clusters of bats hanging upside down, clinging to the rough stone by the claws of their hind feet!

"Phil, you hold two flashlights," the Chief ordered. "Here, Buzz, you hold the bat bands." He handed Buzz two very slender metal rods around which tiny strips of aluminum were bent.

Then he reached up and gently lifted one of the sleeping bats from its roost. With quick deft movements of his fingers, he spread out its wings, took a band off the rod, and slipped it over the front edge of the wing and squeezed it very lightly together. The handling roused the creature, and, giving small squeaks, it reached around with its head to bite the Chief's finger.

The fierce little face looked dangerous, and its tiny white teeth flashed in the beam of the light.

"Doesn't that hurt?" Phil asked in surprise.

"No, its teeth can't even go through your skin," the Chief explained. He put the bat down carefully at one side, and it clumsily flopped along with its wings spread. In a moment it had climbed up the rock wall, then launched

off into flight and disappeared farther into the tunnel.

Working with speed, the Chief wrote the letter *F* next to one of a series of numbers he had in his notebook. He managed to get ten more bats banded before the whole cluster began flying above their heads.

"Look," he said as he held the last specimen.

There, clinging to the animal's underside, was what could only be a tiny, naked baby bat.

"Would you believe it? These little fellows ride around hanging onto their mothers from dusk to dawn for maybe three weeks, until they're big enough to fly by themselves and collect insects to eat."

"What does that *F* you wrote down in your book mean?" Phil asked. "Does it stand for Fletcher?"

His uncle laughed. "No, the *F* is for female, and all the ones I banded today were females. My guess is that they'll all be having babies any day now. The big question is, where can we find the papa bats? I have a hunch they are off in some men's club of their own, and I'd certainly like to find where that club is."

"Say, I don't like that smell," Buzz commented. "Let's go."

There was a strong odor from the bats' bodies, but the

Chief assured them they would get used to it.

"Next year," he went on, "we'll come back and see if the same bats are in the same places. I've noted the exact spot where we found each one I banded. And I wouldn't be surprised if this winter we got some interesting mail. I may hear from the Fish and Wildlife Service that some of these same bats have been captured in Mexico. Nobody knows yet how far south they migrate."

As they emerged from the cave, Phil decided to try an experiment. He nodded toward a wall of red rock and said, "Buzzety-buzzety."

"Buzz-Buzz!" his cousin answered, snapping his fingers.

Phil looked expectantly at the Chief. He wasn't disappointed.

The Chief snapped his fingers and uttered, "Phillity-phillity-phil!"

There was a pause, during which the Chief seemed to expect something more. Tentatively, with a rising inflection, he said, "Chiefety-chiefety-chief?"

The boys roared but refused to give him any satisfaction.

In the coming days they used their clickety-clicks and buzzety-buzzes sparingly, and a couple of times it seemed to Phil that his uncle was going to bust with curiosity, but they carefully gave him no further clues.

The game consoled them a little for their inability to use the Geiger counter. Still, they were impatient.

At last Phil said, "I think we ought to confess we have the Geiger counter. We're wasting a lot of time, climbing all around without it."

"Are you crazy?" Buzz said. "You don't know my pop. He'd be sore because you sneaked behind his back and bought something he told you not to buy."

"*I* sneaked! You mean *we* sneaked."

"All right, *we*. But I'm telling you, he'll make us take it back if he finds out about it."

"Well, doggone it, what *are* we going to do?"

This question was easier asked than answered.

When Phil and Buzz got back to camp on Thursday afternoon, they ran into news that diverted their attention from the Geiger counter problem.

"It's a good thing you weren't home today, Herbert," Aunt Amy said cheerfully. "We had visitors, and you wouldn't have gotten any work done here."

"Isn't that 'Private' sign working?" the Chief asked, bristling.

"Yes and no. First of all, you remember, we expected

Mr. Post to come. This is the day he said he'd bring us some groceries. Well, Mrs. Post came instead. And she's a nice little woman. And then—boys, you'll be interested in this —that man you call The Dinosaur was here."

"No fooling!" Phil exclaimed. "What did he do this time?"

Aunt Amy laughed in a pleasant, relaxed way. "Nothing at all. He just visited with us. He may not be the brightest man in the world, but he's not up to mischief, I'm sure."

"Did you talk to him?" Buzz asked in surprise.

"Didn't he see that 'Private' sign?" the Chief exploded.

"I don't think so. I think he walked down past the place the boys call Rustlers' Fort. Anyway, give me a chance to tell you about him. He's a perfectly harmless character who is trying to set himself up in business. He wants to start a motel somewhere outside the park, maybe in Kanab. So he's trying to find out from tourists just what kind of motel they like and where they would be most likely to stay in one, either coming to the Park or after leaving it. He asked a lot of questions about camping and so on."

"I told you he was crazy," Buzz commented. "What have we got to do with a motel in Kanab? He's nuts."

"Now, Buzz," his mother said, "he has a sensible idea.

He wants to know all about the Park and people who come here, so he can make his plans."

Later Kitsy found a chance to talk to Phil and Buzz privately. "You're right. That man is nuts," she said.

"Tell us everything that happened, Kitsy," Phil urged.

"Well, it was like this," Kitsy began. "Mrs. Post came walking down here in the middle of the morning. She had some strawberries she brought us for a present."

"You didn't eat 'em, did you?" Buzz broke in.

"No, Mommy wouldn't let me have even my share till supper. Anyway, Mrs. Post had some groceries in her car, too—the ones we ordered. But the car was stuck."

"Where? In that hole? We filled the hole in," Buzz said.

"Stop interrupting. She was stuck beside the 'Private' sign. She just couldn't get the engine started, so she walked down the road with the strawberries. She thought the station wagon would be here so we could give her a push. I forgot to tell you, Mr. Post had already gone fishing before she found out that the engine wouldn't work. Mommy and I walked back up the hill with her, and Mommy couldn't start the car, either. So Mrs. Post hitchhiked a ride to the garage, and Mommy and I brought the groceries down to the camp."

"Never mind about Mrs. Post. What about The Dinosaur?" Phil said impatiently.

"Well, I'm *telling* you. When Mommy and I came back here, The Dinosaur was walking around, looking at all of our stuff. Only this time he didn't run away. He just sat down and stayed and asked lots of silly questions."

"What kind of questions?" Phil asked.

"Oh, about what we were doing. I didn't listen."

"Oh, dopey! You should have!" Buzz said. "Maybe you could have found out something important."

"Well, he's crazy, just like you said. Why should I listen to crazy stuff? I don't like him, anyway," Kitsy said positively.

"Where did he go when he left here?" Phil asked.

"He went toward the shortcut past the Rustlers' Fort," Kitsy answered.

"I bet he's spying on us now," Phil said.

All through the evening, while the Chief talked about bats and Aunt Amy played back her tape recordings of bird songs, Phil wondered what was going on out in the dark woods. After he went to bed, he realized that Lulubelle hadn't made her usual appearance. If The Dinosaur was hiding among the trees, maybe he had scared her away.

"I'm going to move this camp and pitch our tents in a nice secluded spot like the lawn in front of the state Capitol in Denver!" the Chief exploded. He was just finishing breakfast and had caught the sound of an engine at the far end of the meadow. "Our 'Private' sign might just as well say 'This way to the circus'!"

"Oh, Daddy, don't be that way," Kitsy said. "It's only the garbage man."

"Then why can't he come when I'm not here?" her father grumbled.

"He did once, and you remember none of us liked it. We thought he was a prowler," Kitsy reminded him.

"Good morning," called the cheerful-looking young driver of the truck. "I have a note for you, Mr. Fletcher."

The Chief opened the envelope that was handed to him,

read the note inside, and passed it to the others. "Blake's a nice fellow. I didn't think he'd impose on me this way," he muttered.

Phil and Buzz looked at the note which said, "Have a big idea that will interest you and the whole family. Bring everybody to my office at 10 A.M. today. No time to explain, but you'll be glad.—Blake."

"It sounds exciting!" Kitsy cried. "Can I take Oliver?"

"Amy, do you think I should go? It means losing a whole day in the field," the Chief said.

"He's been awfully nice to us, Herbert. And he knows how valuable your time is. I'm sure he wouldn't suggest anything foolish."

"Well, all right." The Chief turned to the truck driver. "If you see Blake, tell him we'll meet him at ten o'clock."

"Okay, sir," the young man said. "I'll tell him. I'm going past headquarters on my rounds."

After an hour of spluttering and puttering with small chores, the Chief decided it was about time to start for headquarters. But before he could get everybody into the station wagon, Boyd Blake himself drove up.

"Hi, Chief," the Ranger called out. "I met the garbage truck and heard you want to see me at ten o'clock. I'm going to be busy then, so I thought I'd come right away."

"Somebody's got the cart before the horse," the Chief answered. "You said you wanted to see *me* at ten."

"*I* said?"

"Where's that note, Amy?"

"Why, I guess I tossed it into the campfire," his wife answered.

"Now, let me get this straight," the Ranger said. "You say you got a note from me?"

"The man on the garbage truck brought it," Kitsy said.

"There's some mix-up here," Boyd Blake said. "I didn't send any message."

The Chief told him what the note had said.

"Somebody's playing a practical joke—" the Ranger began, and then he burst out laughing. "I bet I know who did it, and in a way it's your own fault, Chief. The lecture you gave was so good that those kids in the traveling school haven't let me alone for a minute since. They've tried every way they could to see you again. They're plumb full of questions they want to ask you."

"All right!" the Chief roared. "That settles it. I'm going to give them and their teacher what-for! We'll find out from your truck driver which one asked him to deliver the message. What's more, Boyd, I think you ought to take some kind of disciplinary action against them. They've ruined a whole day's work for me."

In a towering rage, the Chief drove out of the meadow behind Boyd Blake.

Phil and Buzz had listened to the uproar in fascinated silence. The practical result was that they had at least an hour or two ahead of them, in which they could do as they liked. It took no time at all to decide what they wanted to do. When Kitsy and her mother were busy, they quietly sneaked the Geiger counter out of their tent, and Phil disappeared with it into the woods. Buzz announced that the two of them were going to take a short hike.

Under cover of the trees, the boys headed toward the edge of the canyon where they had gone the first night they spent in camp. But, before they had gone fifty yards, Buzz who was in the lead stopped and studied the ground intently.

"What you looking at?" Phil asked.

"Footprints. See? Somebody's been here since the big rain we had night before last."

"How do you know?"

"Because that rain would have washed away footprints

that were made before it started."

"Aunt Amy doesn't have a foot that size. You and I didn't make 'em. The Chief's foot is a lot smaller. It must have been The Dinosaur. Kitsy said he used the shortcut from the Fort, but what was he doing down here?"

"Let's see if we can follow his trail," Buzz suggested.

"Hey!" Phil exclaimed after they had picked up another set of tracks farther on. "There's a trail going both ways—toward camp and away from camp!"

A few yards farther along, the soft earth, which still held some moisture from the heavy rain, gave way to a springy mat of grass on which no prints were apparent at all. Still the boys kept on. Obviously whoever had made the tracks preferred the more difficult route through the trees, rather than the easy route across the open meadow. After a long search they found another print, then another. The trail was now turning up the side of the meadow that was opposite the camp. And the footsteps went in both directions. Somebody had gone at least part way around the meadow, hidden by the trees, then retraced his path.

"You know what I think?" Phil asked, and unconsciously his voice dropped to a whisper. "I think that crazy Dinosaur watched our camp after he left yesterday. He just pretended to go up the shortcut and then he sneaked back. But why was he spying on us?"

"Well, he's crazy, isn't he?" Buzz said doubtfully. "So he makes crazy footprints. Or—say, I have another idea. Maybe somebody else was spying on The Dinosaur just because he *is* crazy. They could have been watching him while he was talking to Aunt Amy."

Suddenly Phil had the uncomfortable feeling that he was being watched. It was like the feeling he had had the first day on the trail of the mountain lion, and it made him want to head straight across the meadow. But that was impossible. He and Buzz had to conceal the Geiger counter.

A little nervously, the two of them made a quick trip back through the woods, and when they saw a chance, they ducked into their tent with the machine. Not until then did they discuss whether or not to report the footprints.

"Let's not tell your mother and Kitsy," Phil suggested. "It will just worry them. Let's hike up the road and meet the Chief and tell him, and then we'll decide what to do."

"Check," Buzz said.

With that, they announced their arrival and their departure. "We want to walk up and meet Pop," Buzz said as casually as he could. "Be seeing you."

They were perched on the sawhorse that held their PRIVATE sign when the Chief drove up. One thing they had decided. They simply had to get to the bottom of all the strange things that had happened.

"Can you wait here a minute?" Buzz said. "We want to tell you something before you see Kitsy and Mom."

The Chief listened very seriously to their story. "Now let me tell you something," he said. "The note that came this morning was a pure phony. The traveling school kids left yesterday, although Boyd Blake didn't know it. So they couldn't have sent the note. Last night, or early this morning, somebody attached the envelope, which was addressed to me, to the steering wheel of the garbage truck. The driver hasn't any idea who put it there."

"But why?" Buzz asked. "What was the idea?"

"Don't you see?" Phil said. "Somebody tried to get us all away from camp today. Maybe it was the same person who was hanging around in the woods yesterday."

"The answer may be something like that," the Chief said. "But let me tell you what Boyd Blake and I decided. Now that I hear what you fellows have to report, I'm very sure the decision is right. First, let's not say anything about all this to Kitsy. And you let me talk to Amy about it. Second,

I'm going to stay in camp with them for a while, until we get to the bottom of all this. Third, the Rangers are going to send a man down here to keep an eye on the place, too."

A sense of satisfaction welled up in Phil. Grownups were beginning to see what he and Buzz had known all the time —that something fishy was going on.

"Fourth," the Chief continued, "I'll have plenty of writing to do while I sit in camp, but that will mean you boys won't be occupied—"

"Oh, yes, we will," Phil interrupted. "We can spend all our time doing detective work. We have those footprint clues to start on right away."

"No, fellows, I don't think you'll be needed. The Rangers are going to take care of things like that. Now is the perfect chance for you to take a trip to Phantom Ranch. In fact, I've made reservations for you for tomorrow night. If you want to go by muleback, I can still arrange it that way, but I thought you might prefer to hike down and back."

Confusion swirled in Phil's mind. Here was a wonderful chance to use the Geiger counter for two whole days. But it meant they would miss out on the excitement of tracking down the prowler. The same thoughts were obviously going on in Buzz's head.

"But, Pop, do we *have* to go now?" he protested. "We want to stick around."

"But we want to make the trip, too," Phil added.

"You fellows are certainly hard to please," the Chief said. "I thought you'd jump at the trip."

"Well, Phil, I guess we have to go down the Canyon. It'll be our only chance to use—" Buzz caught himself just in time.

The Chief looked at him with slight suspicion. "To use what?"

"Oh, you know—it's—it'll be fun to hike instead of riding on a mule," Buzz answered vaguely.

"All right, it's agreed," the Chief said. "You can get off to a good early start tomorrow morning."

"Gee, Chief, thanks!" Phil said. "It will be much more fun to hike."

"Just be careful how we talk about the whole plan in front of Kitsy," the Chief warned them. "There's no need to scare her."

Phil and Buzz had no desire to talk about the plan in public. They wanted privacy while they worked out a way of stowing the Geiger counter in a knapsack so that it wouldn't be noticed. Nevertheless, they undertook the job of keeping Kitsy occupied while the Chief told the whole story to his wife.

Then, over supper, the Chief announced that the boys were going to hike down into the Canyon.

"It's no fair!" Kitsy burst out. "Why can't I go? The boys have all the fun. You haven't even taken me on a bat trip. I could help you just as well as they can, and I'm getting tired of only helping Mommy watch her birds."

"Don't worry, Kitsy, you'll have a trip down into the Canyon later," her father said. "And I've been planning to ask if you wouldn't go on a bat trip. I didn't know you really wanted to."

Kitsy seemed satisfied, and Buzz saw a chance to break away from the table. "Phil, let's go and get our stuff together," he mumbled, starting toward the tent.

"You'd better do just that," Aunt Amy said. "I peeked in your tent today and it's a scandalous mess. How you'll ever find anything, I don't know."

A moment or two later, her voice came to them: "If you boys will collect your dirty clothes, I'll wash them for you while you're gone."

"That's the frosting on the cake!" Phil called back. "Thanks! Here come the dirty socks!"

And the socks literally came flying out, as the two boys did a double-quick cleanup job.

"For goodness' sake! Put that stuff in your laundry bag!" Aunt Amy exclaimed.

Phil groaned. He simply couldn't understand why she thought he should go through the tedious and unnecessary step of putting things into the bag when they would only have to be taken out again on washday.

Presently Buzz extracted a knapsack from a shapeless heap of junk at the foot of his bedroll. "Where's your knapsack, Phil? We better start figuring how we're going to pack the Geiger counter."

"It's in that pile somewhere. You look for it," Phil answered. At the same time he pulled the counter out from under his sleeping bag and tested it for size in Buzz's knapsack. It made a very obvious squarish lump.

"We'll have to wrap it up so the corners won't show," he said.

Finally they worked out a plan for wrapping the Geiger counter in a sweater. The earphones were in the bathing trunks that the Chief had said they would need when they went swimming in the pool at Phantom Ranch.

They finished the job none too soon, for the Chief came

to the door of the tent and asked, "How are you coming along?"

"Aw, Chief, we're doing all right. Don't worry," Buzz protested.

"For goodness' sake, Herbert! Let them alone. They're old enough to do things for themselves," Aunt Amy called.

The Chief picked up Phil's knapsack and exclaimed, "What in the world do you have in here? It feels like a ton of bricks."

"Oh, canteens and stuff," Buzz answered quickly.

"Do you realize that you're going to walk fourteen miles down tomorrow? And then fourteen miles back up the next day?"

"Don't worry!" Buzz protested again.

His father shrugged. "It's no skin off my shoulder blades, but I advise you to travel lighter than this."

It had been a close call, and they sighed with relief when they crawled into their sleeping bags at last.

Thinking it all over, Phil didn't feel too badly about postponing his search for the cause of the strange happenings around camp. Somehow he was perfectly certain that the Chief and the Rangers on guard would not discover anything important.

17 AGAINST REGULATIONS

"Amy, why don't you and Kitsy take the boys in the station wagon to the head of the trail?" the Chief said after breakfast. "I have a lot of work to do on my notes."

Phil and Buzz knew that this had been planned ahead of time, although it sounded casual. The Chief didn't want to leave his wife and Kitsy alone in camp. The boys were delighted with the suggestion for a reason all their own. Aunt Amy wouldn't think of prying into their knapsacks at the last minute.

In the fresh, cool air of the morning she drove them to the place where the Kaibab Trail started down toward Bright Angel Canyon. Now, for two blessed days, they would be on their own.

The broad trail switched back and forth down the steep, wooded slope at an easy grade, and they were very soon out of sight of Kitsy and her mother.

As soon as they knew that it was safe, Phil reached into his cousin's pack and took out the Geiger counter.

"Wait a minute," he said, before putting on the earphones. Without a word, he took off his own pack, fished out a full canteen of water, and stuffed it into the empty space left by the removal of the counter. "Gotta even up the load," he said with a grin.

"Well, doggone you!" Buzz said.

Phil just kept grinning and put on the earphones. Then he pushed the switch and walked slowly along, with the counter held close to the rocks that jutted out on the uphill side of the trail. The background count of the machine sounded exciting at first. But after a while it grew monotonous. There was no perceptible variation in it.

"It's my listen now," Buzz demanded presently.

This called for a conference.

"We're going to wear these batteries out, if we're not careful," Phil said thoughtfully as he relinquished the machine. "That red-colored rock that looks like the Vermilion Cliffs is where we'd better concentrate." He glanced down the canyon wall, which was growing steadily steeper. On one side, far below them, they saw the broad band of deep red rock. It was one of the many thick layers of different kinds of rock that lay exposed between the top and the bottom of the canyon.

"But we might find stuff sooner," Buzz protested.

"And we might not have any juice in the batteries when we get to the real good stuff, either," Phil answered. "I'll tell you what—we have to come back up this same way. You listen for just a minute. Then let's hightail down to the red stuff. Tomorrow we can do this top part of the canyon on the way home. If we've got any juice left."

"We sure were dopes not to buy an extra battery," Buzz commented.

"You mean we sure were dopes not to have money enough for one."

"Never mind. We won't have to worry about money when we strike it rich."

Both of them agreed on this obvious truth. And they hurried down the trail.

"Boy, we're getting there!" Buzz said presently. "You want to take it now? It's your turn, I guess."

Phil quickly fitted the earphones over his head, took the small box in his hand, and swung along the trail as fast as he could walk. At the first showing of red sandstone, he turned the switch and held the counter close to the gritty surface of a rock. He heard only the background click and frugally turned off the switch.

"You know, we're crazy," he said. "If there's any uranium along the trail here, somebody would have found it already. I bet a thousand people have gone up and down with counters. We have to get *off* the trail."

This was easier said than done. The forest that blanketed the top of the plateau had disappeared, and the footpath wound through bare rocks that thrust up crazily. But at the end of a switchback they saw a chance to explore on a slope that seemed to offer stable footing.

As Phil stepped out, Buzz shouted, "Take care of that counter. Don't bang it and break it."

Phil nodded. But he felt uneasy for several reasons. The slope was dangerous and he had only one hand free. And it was against Park regulations to leave the trail. Neither he nor Buzz wanted to mention this unpleasant fact. Uranium fever had got them, and they were determined to go on.

At last, on a flat stretch of rock where he felt safe, Phil turned the switch and almost rubbed the little box over the exposed surface of the sandstone. Suddenly, he knew that something was happening! The clicks came faster and faster. Or was he just imagining it? No! The farther he pushed the box to the right, the more clicks he heard. This might be it—an uranium strike.

"Wow! She's gone crazy! We found it!" he shouted.

Buzz reached for the box. Surprised, Phil stepped back and almost lost his balance. He felt his cousin grab his arm and pull him toward the face of the rock.

"What's the idea?" Phil blurted out.

Buzz simply pointed a shaking hand downward. Words weren't necessary. One glance told Phil how close he had come to falling fifty feet or more—straight down.

Limply Phil sagged with his back tight against the rock, and Buzz eased himself to a sitting position beside him. As Phil began to recover, he was aware of a roar filling his ears. It was the pounding of his heart, but along with it came the rapid click-click of the counter. Slowly he pulled the earphones off and handed them to Buzz.

"You want 'em?" he mumbled.

Buzz had largely recovered from his sudden fright, but his movements were cautious as he took the box and put on the phones.

The two boys slid gingerly past each other, and now Buzz

stood where Phil had been when he thought he got a high count. Then Buzz's shoulders hunched up in tenseness and his knees bent a little as he waved the box out ahead of him along the rock face. Fearing that Buzz, in his excitement, might forget the danger, Phil reached out and grabbed his belt and firmly drew Buzz toward him. Then he signaled him to take off the earphones.

"Boy! We made our strike! Did you hear her click?"

"Did I hear!"

"Wait till we tell Pop," Buzz said gleefully. "Won't he feel like a dope for saying we couldn't have a counter!"

"Did you turn the switch off?" Phil asked.

Buzz had forgotten, and reluctantly shut off the little rattling sound that was the sweetest music he had ever heard. "Shall we go right now and tell Pop, or shall we do a little more prospecting first?" he asked.

"We don't *have* to do any more. We found it," Phil answered. "All we have to do is put up a marker here and it's our mining claim. The only thing is, we have to be careful that nobody jumps the claim and steals it from us."

"How do we do that?" Buzz was a little bit alarmed.

"I don't know exactly. There are ways. Your Pop or Boyd Blake will tell us what to do."

"Well, let's get going. Boy, is the Grand Canyon going to be famous!"

But Phil was having second thoughts. "Wait a minute. We'd better not tell the Chief or Boyd Blake or *anybody* about this until we're sure we've got everything fixed up so we really own it."

"How are we going to have a mine here if we don't tell anyone?" Buzz asked. "But you're right about the Chief. There are all kinds of reasons why we can't go back and tell him this minute. He's all worked up because of this prowler, and that would just make him madder because we bought the Geiger counter behind his back. Also, he's already paid for our room and board at Phantom Ranch tonight. All that money would be wasted, just when he thought he was being so generous. No, *sir!*"

Phil hated to give up the possibility of having his cake and eating it, too. Now that they had found their uranium mine, it was a shame not to go back and have the fun of tracking the prowler.

"Well," Phil said, "maybe we could sneak back and live at Rustlers' Fort for two days. We have some food, and we could stay there keeping an eye on camp at least."

"Are you crazy? The Rangers would find us. Then they

would say *we* were the prowlers. And the Chief would believe them."

Phil knotted his forehead in bewilderment and frustration. "Shucks!" he said.

"What's the good of taking a chance?" Buzz went on. "We have to have time to think, anyway. And we can think as we hike along. Nothing is going to happen to our mine in two days. This uranium has been here for a billion years and it will be here a little while longer."

"Oh, all right," Phil agreed reluctantly. Then he began to cheer up, now that a decision had been reached. "You know what? That guy in Kanab where we bought the Geiger counter will know exactly what we have to do about our mining claim. We just have to be careful not to tell him where we made the strike."

"Sure. Now we better figure out how we're going to locate this particular place again."

Both boys studied the confused mass of red and orange and gray rocks, looking for landmarks. Phil traced the zigzags of the trail down which they had come. Then, "Hey, we'd better scram! There are some people up there. They'll see us if we don't hurry. Maybe they've seen us already."

Moving as rapidly as they dared, they headed for the trail.

"All these doggone switchbacks look alike," Buzz said. "How are we going to know where to turn off for our mine?"

Phil saw a flat slab of sandstone just off the trail at a point where it made a sharp turn. "Here," he said. "We'll pile some rocks on top of this flat place. Nobody but us will know what they mean."

Together they made a neat little pyramid of stones, surveyed it from a distance, and were sure they could find it again.

"Now let's light out of here. Those tourists are getting closer. And besides, Pop said we should get down to Bright Angel Creek by lunchtime. I feel like it's lunchtime already —and I'm thirsty!"

They took drinks from their canteens and swung on down the trail at a fast clip. Several times Phil stopped and tried the Geiger counter on interesting-looking rocks that they passed. But none of the formations produced the exciting clicks in his ears. The sun beat down with ferocity. The last tree seemed miles behind them, but below they could see a ribbon of green where Bright Angel Creek flowed. At one point the trail forked. To the left, a quarter of a mile away, Phil saw a beautiful, tempting cascade of water that came surprisingly out of a dark hole in the canyon wall and filled the dry air with its refreshing sparkle and rumble.

"Roaring Springs," Phil read on the sign at the side of the trail. "They sure got the right name for it!"

"Let's go and have a look," Buzz suggested.

But Phil shook his head. "That's a side trip. We've still got about nine miles to go, boy, and we lost a lot of time discovering the mine. We better hike right on if we want to reach the Ranch in time for supper."

Silently they took the right fork in the trail and plodded on downhill. Their spirits rose when they came on a sudden burst of green vegetation around a big, fat, wooden pipeline. Water under great pressure spurted out at crazy angles through leaks in the pipe and provided a perpetual shower to the plants that grew near it. Apparently the pipe came from Roaring Springs and brought water to turn the machinery that generated electricity for the hotel and Park headquarters far above on the Canyon rim. Soon they could hear the deep hum of the generators that were housed in a small modern building. Near it stood a house that they guessed was used by the person who took care of the power plant. It gave Phil a queer sensation to come on this tiny bit of civilization in the midst of such a vast and barren wilderness.

But more interesting than the power plant was the creek that ran just below it. A sudden passionate desire to do something he hadn't done since he was a little kid swept over Phil. He wanted to go wading. No—not wading. He just wanted to sit on the bank and dangle his hot feet in the water. In a minute he was seated on a shady rock with shoes and socks off, and his toes wriggled sensuously as the clear, icy water poured over them. From the bare feet, new energy seemed to flow upward through his whole body.

Then he realized that he didn't have to be as uncomfortable as he was. He had been wearing the earphones for miles, it seemed, although the Geiger counter which he carried in his hand hadn't been turned on for a long way.

He was just laying the earphones aside when a voice said, "Hiyah, fellows. Having a good trip?"

Phil and Buzz looked up in surprise. The noise of the rushing water had drowned out any sound of approaching footsteps. There stood a wiry middle-aged man with a face deeply tanned and a friendly air about him.

"Yeah, wonderful," Buzz answered. "This Canyon is bigger than I ever thought it was."

"Going all the way to Phantom Ranch?" the man asked.

"Sure. We're going to spend the night there."

Buzz had his feet out of the water now. He opened his packsack and removed a bundle of sandwiches. "Want some of our lunch?" he asked the stranger.

"Thanks, I've got my own." The man sat down on a rock and pulled a cardboard box out of a canvas bag he carried at his side.

Phil was relieved that he and Buzz didn't have to part with any of their lunch, which looked very small compared to the enormous appetite he had worked up.

"It's none of my business," the stranger said, "but I see you've got a Geiger counter. Are you prospecting?"

"Yeah," Phil answered.

"Did any Rangers see you fellows on your way down?"

Phil looked at him sharply and wondered what he had on his mind. "Not that I know of."

"Well, let me give you a tip then. In case you don't know it, the Rangers don't allow prospecting in the Park. If anybody sees you, you'll probably get into a lot of trouble."

Both boys were flabbergasted. "Are you kidding?" Buzz asked.

"Indeed not!" the man answered. "I just had a hunch

you didn't know about the regulations or you would have kept your machine out of sight."

"But they have uranium mines all over—down by the Vermilion Cliffs," Phil said.

"I know, but that's outside the Park," the man explained. "I'd advise you to put that thing away and keep it out of sight, so you won't get into any arguments with anybody."

Hastily, Phil opened his knapsack and packed the Geiger counter away. "Thanks, mister, for telling us," he said. "We sure didn't know about any such rule."

"Did you pick up any signs of radioactivity?" the man asked with friendly curiosity. "I've heard there are plenty of places in this desert country where you can locate small pockets of radioactive ore."

Phil was inclined to feel cautious. But Buzz blurted out, "Yeah, we found one place. Are you sure it won't do us any good?"

"Let me ask another question first. How old are you kids?"

This made Phil feel even more cautious. The man was certainly nosy about their business. Buzz, too, kept his council.

"I'd make a guess at sixteen," the stranger continued.

The flattery was too much for Buzz. He enjoyed being taken for a year older than he actually was. "Wrong," he said with a grin. "We're both fifteen."

"Then I'll tell you something else that may save you some heartaches," said the stranger. "You have to be twenty-one before you can stake out a claim in your own name. So you better take some grownup in as a partner."

Phil had a sudden suspicion that the man was trying to chisel a share of the uranium they had discovered. As if the stranger could read Phil's mind, he smiled and said, "Don't worry, I'm not in the market. Mining's not my line."

Phil wondered what his line was, but he wanted the conversation to end as quickly as possible. It had proved much too uncomfortable. Bleakly, he began to wish he had let the Chief talk him out of spending his money on a Geiger counter. Now the money was gone, and he had lost a uranium mine, too. It would have been better—much better—if they had stayed in camp and worked on the mysterious footprints. Now the Rangers and the Chief would have two days in which to catch The Dinosaur or whoever was prowling around. Things might be all settled by the time they got home. Why did everything have to be such a mess?

18

For eight intensely hot miles Phil scarcely noticed the vast cliffs that towered on either side of the narrow canyon down which Bright Angel Creek flowed. At another time he might have been amazed to find signs that beaver lived in this unlikely spot. He might have stood and watched lizards crawling up the hot rocks. But the afternoon was filled only with worry. Wasn't there *some* way they could keep their uranium mine? Had the stranger really told them the truth? How could they find out? The man who had sold them the Geiger counter in Kanab would probably know all the rules. But when would they make another trip to the town? Meantime, they would have to keep on hiding the machine from the Chief.

"Doggone the Chief, anyway," Phil burst out. "He could have told us the Park has a rule against Geiger counters."

"He didn't know it, I bet," Buzz said a little belligerently. "Why not?"

"Do you expect him to know *everything*? I'm sure he never heard of this Park rule. He gave us what he thought were perfectly good reasons why we shouldn't buy a Geiger counter. The rule isn't his fault, so don't go blaming him."

Phil didn't want to argue any more. His feet were getting sore. The only pleasant moments in the afternoon were the half-dozen times when the trail switched back and forth across the creek. Each time he and Buzz took off their shoes and socks and waded—and felt refreshed. After a while the canyon grew still narrower. The dark, gloomy walls pressed in on Phil from both sides, and all the sunlight and heat that entered the yawning space above him seemed to funnel down right on top of his head.

When signs on the winding path indicated that Phantom Ranch lay only a little way ahead, Phil decided not to bother taking off shoes and socks. He just sloshed through the water and went on.

"You'll be sorry," Buzz warned him.

Phil didn't believe him. But the last stretch of trail into the Ranch was torture. The damp socks bunched inside his shoes. The moisture made his skin tender and sensitive.

He could scarcely hobble when a little cluster of buildings came into view.

There, in a kind of farmyard, three men squatted in the shade of a big cottonwood tree. Two were cowboys and the third seemed to be a Ranger; at least he had on a Ranger's hat. Dull as Phil was with fatigue, he did a double take. Had that stranger they met at lunchtime phoned down and squealed on the boys? Was the Ranger waiting to nab them for prospecting?

Apparently not. He greeted them and asked if they had had a good trip.

"Are you the two young fellows who have reservations for tonight?" one of the cowboys asked.

Again Phil was suspicious. How did this bird know so much about him and Buzz? Nevertheless, he nodded.

"Come on, I'll show you to your cabin."

Somewhat relieved and reassured, the boys stumbled along after him. In their cabin they scarcely looked around, and when their guide was gone, they flopped down on their beds without even taking off their shoes. A moment later there came a knock on the screen door.

"Forgot to tell you," the cowboy said. "When the bell rings it's suppertime. But you do have time for a swim."

After a while Phil revived. "Do you hear what I hear?" he asked. A noisy splashing and laughter came from out in front of their cabin. "Get into your swimming trunks."

By the time they reached the edge of the pear-shaped swimming pool that had been built in the center of the circle of cabins, several tourists of all ages, sizes, and shapes were soaking lazily in the water. Apparently they had come down by muleback either from the North Rim of the Canyon or from the South Rim, across the river.

Phil lay back languidly and floated with arms outstretched and eyes half closed. He drifted toward one edge of the pool, and when his hand touched the rough masonry rim, he opened his eyes wide to get his bearings. All of a sudden his muscles tensed at what he saw, and he sank, to come up spluttering. A second look confirmed his fears. There, sitting in a folding camp chair close to the edge of the pool—and watching him—was The Dinosaur.

This time the man didn't have on a business suit. Instead he wore blue jeans, and the small head on top of his long neck was covered with a Stetson. But there was no mistaking him. It was the same queer-looking fellow who had turned up in so many queer places in the last couple of weeks.

Phil turned on his stomach and swam with long easy

strokes to the other side of the pool where Buzz was about ready to dive from the edge.

"Come on, we got to get out of here," Phil said urgently.

Inside the cabin, with the screen door closed, Phil told Buzz to look at the big man on the other side of the pool.

"The Dinosaur!" Buzz gasped. "What—what—"

"He must have followed us. Nothing else makes any sense. He must have come with that party on muleback."

"I don't like it," Buzz said. "What are we going to do?"

The clatter of a bell broke in.

"Yipe! Dinner! Get your clothes on—I'm starved."

They flung on clean shirts, then hurried out. Ahead of them trudged a dozen or fifteen tourists, most of them waddling stiffly and with legs spread in a way that could only show they had spent the day in the saddle—and that they weren't used to riding mules. The Dinosaur's waddle was proof that he had come down by muleback.

Fortunately the waitress showed Phil and Buzz to a different table from the one where The Dinosaur sat. It seemed strange to be having a civilized meal after three weeks of camping, and strangest of all to be eating it in such an unlikely place as the bottom of the Grand Canyon.

"I bet you we don't get enough," Phil whispered to Buzz.

"An ordinary restaurant's bad enough."

"What can you expect?" Buzz answered. "They have to bring all the stuff down from the top of the Canyon on pack mules."

But it wasn't long before their worries were forgotten. After the first helpings of steak, mashed potatoes, beets, hot biscuits, salad, jams, relishes, and olives, the waitress appeared from the kitchen with seconds.

The boys were so absorbed in the important task of getting food while it lasted that they didn't notice a conspiracy developing among the older people who sat on both sides of their long table. Time and again the biscuit plate was passed to them, then the steak platter, then the bowls of vegetables. Politely Phil and Buzz helped themselves each time the dishes went past, and the dishes came with increasing frequency. As they began to eat a little more slowly, Phil looked up and realized with a slight feeling of self-consciousness that every bowl and platter on the table was ranged in front of him and Buzz. And all the grownups were eagerly watching as if the boys were racers about to establish a world record.

"Won't you have a little more steak, son—to take the edge off your appetite?" said a middle-aged man.

Phil grinned and reached for an olive. "I think this one olive will just about do me."

The waitress brought in stewed fruit and a cake. By now the boys had begun to enjoy the jokes that the adults kept tossing in their direction. By the time they had finished the meal, they discovered that the people at the other table had already gotten up and departed.

Heavily, uncomfortably, Phil and Buzz eased themselves down the steps outside the dining room. While the older people either went to their cabins or found camp chairs outside, the boys flopped down with genuine groans and lay flat on their backs on the grass. For half an hour they rested and recovered from their mammoth feast. At first they were too stuffed to talk about The Dinosaur.

Buzz was the first to feel a spark of returning life. "What do you think that crazy guy is up to, following us around everywhere and watching us?"

"Do you suppose it could just possibly be an accident that he keeps turning up all the time?" Phil wondered.

"I don't see how. It's happened too many times."

"What can we do about him?" Phil asked.

"Not a thing. He hasn't done anything to *us*. At least, we can't prove that he has. Let's forget it and go down to see the river. We'd better do it tonight, so we can get an early start up the trail tomorrow morning," Buzz suggested.

Unenthusiastically, Phil agreed and heaved himself to his feet. As long as he had come this far, he guessed he ought to go a half mile farther, so that he could say he had actually seen the Colorado River.

Slowly the two of them walked along the broad trail that led from the Ranch, down Bright Angel Creek, to the river. When they reached the point where the crystal clear water of the creek poured into the muddy river, they stopped in amazement. Phil thought he had never seen anything that seemed to have such enormous, terrifying power as the rushing, turbulent brown water that swept by at express-train speed. Occasional fountains shot up into the air, as the current struck boulders deep beneath the surface. Now and then a deep thump of boulder striking boulder punctuated the steady roar of the rushing river.

"Boy, I begin to see how the Colorado *could* chew its way down through all this rock," Phil said.

The awful spectacle gave both of them a certain feeling of uneasiness, and in Phil's mind it brought worry about The Dinosaur to the surface.

"Maybe—he's some kind of uranium spy. Or maybe he's

a government guy—looking for prospectors who aren't supposed to be prospecting!" Phil said.

"That doesn't seem right, because he started hanging around us before we bought the Geiger counter."

"Maybe it's his job to keep an eye on just about everybody. A lot of people probably get the idea of hunting for uranium where they aren't supposed to hunt."

"Well, if the government is all that particular, why don't they tell you so in big letters when you come into the Park?"

"I don't know, but I don't like that guy."

"Neither do I. Well, we're not doing anything we shouldn't right now, so let's look at the swinging bridge."

They wandered on down the trail a hundred yards, toward the bridge on which mule parties from the South Rim crossed over the river. After they had stepped out on it a little way, they stopped by mutual consent. The swaying of the flimsy-looking structure added to their uneasiness.

"How do they get ornery critters like mules to walk over this thing?" Phil wondered.

"Well, they do. Let's go. We ought to get back before it's dark," Buzz proposed and Phil readily agreed.

Phil turned. The Dinosaur's big body was blocking the end of the bridge. He had obviously followed them to the river, and they couldn't get back to the Ranch without passing him—at a place where one shove would send anybody plunging into the torrent below. Sudden panic rose up in Phil. Maybe they should run across to the other side of the bridge.

"Let's just go by him as if everything's all right," Buzz whispered. "He better not try anything funny." But his voice didn't sound as brave as his words.

"Some river, isn't it?" The Dinosaur's voice startled them.

"Sure is," Phil said and brushed past him.

"Your folks still camped up on top?" The man was talking at the boys' backs now.

"Yeah," Buzz said without turning.

They hurried up the trail. "Whew! That was a close one," Buzz panted.

"Well, anyway, he didn't try anything. I tell you, he *is* spying. Following us and then asking us about our camp!"

"He's coming after us now!" Buzz had turned and glanced back.

But the big man was no match for the boys. They reached their cabin long before he hobbled into the Ranch area.

Phil made sure the screen door was locked before they went to bed. It was too hot to close the door itself.

19

Phil and Buzz were in no mood to put on another marathon eating exhibition at breakfast. But they did hastily stow away second helpings of bacon, scrambled eggs, and pancakes. And they noticed with relief that The Dinosaur had apparently slept late. He wasn't at the other table.

"Let's scram before that guy sees us," Phil proposed.

They were up from the table and out of the dining room before any of the other guests had finished eating. As they approached the line of identical cabins Phil glanced along the row to pick out theirs—Number 9. A motion he saw through the window of Number 9 caught his eye. He stopped. Somebody was in their cabin.

A few steps closer and he could see a man clearly silhouetted between the window on the near side and the window on the far side. There was no question who it was.

Now Buzz had seen the same thing. With one accord, they ducked down and sneaked along the cabin wall. In a moment the two of them were looking cautiously over the lower edge of the far window. The Dinosaur's back was toward them, but they could see clearly what he was doing. He was rummaging through Phil's knapsack on the bed. A slight noise made him straighten up suddenly.

The screen door opened, and in came a man with an armload of clean sheets, pillowcases, and towels.

"Good morning," The Dinosaur said with composure. "These cabins all look alike. I came in here thinking it was Number seven."

"Next door," the linen man grunted and held the screen open for The Dinosaur to go out.

When he had disappeared into his own cabin, the boys hurried around the opposite side of theirs. Inside they paused for a moment, then slung their packs on their backs and were out of the place. Phil knew without asking that Buzz and he had the same idea; they had better head for home right away. The more distance between them and The Dinosaur the better.

As soon as they had left the last Ranch building well behind them, Buzz said, "He's a crook, all right. He must have seen us yesterday using our Geiger counter and he was going to swipe it. Boy, were we lucky!"

"If we just hurry up and get to the top of the trail in time we can tell Boyd Blake to arrest him."

"Hey, we're crazy! We ought to go back and tell the Ranger at the Ranch," Buzz said, stopping abruptly.

"Not by a long shot!" Phil answered. "The Ranger would tell us to open up our packs and see if anything was missing, and then he'd see the Geiger counter. Uh-*uh!*"

"Well, then we can't tell Boyd Blake, either," Buzz said.

"Sure, we can hide it and then tell him."

"Oh, no we can't," Buzz said dismally. "When The Dinosaur is arrested, he'll squeal on us. He'll say we were using the counter and breaking the law, and then he'll seem like a good guy who was just trying to get the evidence on us so he could report us to the Ranger."

Phil looked up at the seemingly endless climb that lay ahead. If there was any escape from being caught with the illegal Geiger counter, it lay in reaching the rim of the canyon, and then going to Kanab as fast as possible so they could sell the fascinating, troublesome machine.

At first Phil's muscles were stiff and sore from the previous day's hike, but they loosened up quickly as he swung along at a fast walk. Surprisingly, his feet which had been tender the night before were in good shape. Today, crossing the stream, he dutifully removed his shoes and socks every time. He had been thirsty yesterday, but today his thirst seemed twice as great. At every crossing of the creek, he and Buzz gulped up some of the sweet, cool water, but the only rest they took was when they sat down to remove or put on their shoes. Nor did they waste much breath talking.

It was well before noon when they approached the power-house on Bright Angel Creek where they had eaten lunch the day before.

Lunch!

"Are we the prize dopes of the century!" Buzz moaned. "Do you know what we did this morning? We got so excited about The Dinosaur that we forgot to pick up our lunch boxes!"

It was routine at Phantom Ranch to supply each overnight guest with a box lunch.

"Why didn't you say something before we got too far away?" Phil demanded angrily.

"Why didn't *you* say something, stupid?"

"Rats!" Phil was furious—and suddenly so hungry that he didn't think he could stand it. Then he grew worried.

By far the hardest part of the climb lay ahead, and they would need every ounce of energy to keep going.

"Hey, have we still got that hunk of chocolate Pop gave us for emergencies?" Buzz asked.

"I don't know. Let's have a look." Phil poked around in the knapsack on Buzz's back. No sign of the chocolate. Then he turned around to have his own pack inspected.

"Great day in the morning!" Buzz exploded with relief.

He fished out a big bar of semi-sweet chocolate which in spite of the intense heat had not gone soft and gooey the way sweet chocolate would have. It tasted bitter, but it was mightily welcome.

"We better save some till later on," Buzz said.

Reluctantly Phil saw the wisdom of this. They put half of the bar away, filled their canteens, and headed upward. This would be their last chance to get water until they reached a tiny spring miles away.

Now they were gaining altitude rapidly. The trail switched back and forth on the precipitous canyon side. Their fast pace and the steady climb were beginning to tell on them. Buzz was in the lead, and as they reached the end of one switchback, he called out, panting deeply, "Phil, I got to rest a minute."

The blood was pounding in Phil's temples, sweat poured down his cheeks, and his shirt clung to him as if he had been in a rainstorm. To ease his aching legs, he turned and faced downhill. There was encouragement to be gained in looking at the long stretch of trail they had already covered. But his feeling of achievement soon gave way to alarm. Moving steadily along this side of the Roaring Springs turnoff, was a string of mules. One of the riders must surely be The Dinosaur.

They hurried on. As the trail continued to climb, the air became thinner and their breathing grew more labored. At brief stops they took frugal swigs of water from their canteens. The last of it was gone long before they reached a little pool into which a spring dripped slowly from moss on an overhanging ledge. A giant pinnacle of rock furnished shade for them here. They refilled the canteens, finished the chocolate, and resumed what now had become a race against the mules.

These tough animals, which had made the same trip perhaps hundreds of times, seemed to press on relentlessly behind them. They could see the party more clearly now. There was one big figure among the riders, wearing a Stetson hat, and Phil was sure it must be The Dinosaur.

Indecision and dismay held them for a moment when they reached the place where they had left the marker for their uranium strike.

"Do you suppose we've got time to go over and break off a sample of that rock to show the guy in Kanab?" Phil asked.

"What good would it do us? Then they'd have some real evidence on us. Let's get out of here!" Buzz's voice was dry and thin with exhaustion.

More and more frequently now, they had the blessed shade of trees which spread down from the top of the Kaibab Plateau, and great masses of clouds began to stand between the boys and the sun.

"*Now* we got clouds!" Buzz said sourly. "Why couldn't it blow up a storm when we were down below, where the trees don't grow?"

When the sudden gush of rain came out of the sky, it refreshed them a little and they slogged on feeling somewhat more comfortable. Then they got chilly. Before long, rivulets began to run down the trail, and their feet started to slip in the mud.

The rain stopped as suddenly as it had started, and through openings in the trees they could catch glimpses of the trail below. The mules were coming closer. Only a few switchbacks separated them from the boys. Every step Phil took now required intense, painful effort. He could see that Buzz walked clumsily, almost staggering.

Then at last the trail heaved over the top of the canyon rim, and ahead of them lay the parking lot. This was where the Chief had agreed to be at five o'clock, but there was no sign of him.

In a husky voice, Phil asked, "What time do you think it is?"

Neither of them had a watch. "I don't know and I don't care," Buzz answered. "Just let me sit down."

"Not here," Phil said. "Those mules will pass here any minute. Let's get out of sight."

Painfully they went over a little hillock where they could raise their heads and keep an eye on the parking lot without being seen. They flopped down on the damp earth and had their first moment of real rest since they left the creek hours before.

It was a surprisingly long time before the mules actually put in an appearance. But when they did, the boys got some small pleasure out of watching The Dinosaur slide painfully off the big animal that carried him. After a word with the guide, he hobbled stiffly over to his Ford, unlocked it, and sat down gingerly behind the wheel. He had been gone from the parking lot only a few minutes when the Fletchers' station wagon turned in.

"Whoof! Am I glad to see that old buggy!" Buzz sighed.

"Have a good time?" the Chief called brightly as the boys approached.

"Yeah," Buzz answered hoarsely but without enthusiasm.

His father grinned. "You two look as if you'd been drawn through a knothole. Get in. You can tell about it after you've had some hot supper."

Exhausted though he was, Phil had enough energy left to ask one question: "Did you catch the prowler?"

"We didn't even catch cold," the Chief answered cheerfully. "If there was any trouble around, it's all over now. The fact is, we all feel a little bit silly."

"But what about that mysterious note you got, telling you to come to Boyd Blake's office?" Buzz croaked.

"Oh, that!" the Chief laughed heartily. "Somebody was playing a practical joke on Boyd, not on me. They put notes like that on half a dozen different automobiles in the Park, and all day long people kept coming in for appointments with Boyd that he'd never heard about. He doesn't know which one of his friends pulled the stunt, but he's sure sore, and he's going to find out."

"What about the footprints we found?" Phil asked.

"They didn't prove anything by themselves. And you know there *are* hundreds of tourists in the Park all the time. Even though we are in an isolated spot, somebody wandered around in the woods. That's all."

Phil wasn't at all convinced, but he was too tired to think or talk any more. With only half an ear, he listened as the Chief rattled on with other news of the happenings at camp during the last two days. Lulubelle had knocked over the garbage can once more. Oliver had climbed a tree and had been an awful nuisance to get down. Mr. Post had dropped by for a minute on his way down Dry Bones Canyon to fish. They were going to spend every day next week banding bats, because they didn't have to go to Kanab.

"What?" Phil croaked. "I thought we were going in a few days."

"That was the plan, but we don't have to now. I found that one of the bus drivers will do our shopping for us whenever we want, so we can stay here on the job."

It seemed to Phil as if he had been strapped into a strait jacket and then set down on a box of dynamite. He and

Buzz would somehow have to keep on hiding that Geiger counter until they could find a way to go to Kanab and get rid of it. He couldn't enjoy a peaceful minute until he had disposed of the evidence that he had done exactly what he had been told not to do—and on top of it had broken a bunch of government rules, which maybe made sense although he couldn't see why.

Buzz was obviously thinking along the same line. At the first chance, after they reached camp, he whispered, "Phil, what are you going to do about your Geiger counter?"

"*My* Geiger counter? It's ours!"

"Well, you put up twenty and I only put up two," Buzz said.

"I loaned you nine dollars, you mean."

"Well, you can have that back. You can have the two dollars, too. I don't care anymore."

"No, sirree-bob, you're in this as much as I am. You got to take half the blame—and you owe me nine dollars, even if we can't get anything back on the counter. Maybe it was spoiled in the rain."

"Hey, Phil, you're taking me seriously," Buzz said with genuine concern in his voice. "I thought you realized I was only kidding. We're in this together, boy!"

"Guess what's for supper!" Kitsy said to the boys as soon as they emerged from their tent after changing into dry clothes and hiding the Geiger counter.

Phil sniffed a wonderful, unfamiliar odor that came from a frying pan on the gasoline stove.

"Trout! Fresh trout!" Kitsy answered her own question. "We've got one apiece. Mr. Post gave 'em to us."

Phil and Buzz stuffed themselves with bread and butter while they waited for the trout to finish cooking. Only after they had eaten the delicate flesh of the fish, along with potatoes, heaps of bacon, and other things, did they answer any questions about their trip. Then they relaxed, and first one, then the other, told censored bits of their experiences in the Canyon. Once Phil caught himself on the verge of mentioning The Dinosaur, and for a while he let

Buzz do the reporting. As he half-listened, an idea was shaping itself in his mind.

Interrupting Buzz, Phil asked, "Aunt Amy, did Mr. Post say whether they caught the guy who robbed his store?"

"No, they haven't found him yet," she answered.

Phil lapsed into silence again. He would bet a hundred dollars that The Dinosaur was the robber. Phil and Buzz had absolute proof that the guy was a crook: He had been rifling their packsacks at Phantom Ranch. Things were beginning to add up!

Trying to keep the excitement from his voice, Phil blurted out, "I'm bushed. Let's hit the sack, Buzz."

Buzz admitted that he, too, was done in. But, once in the tent, he revived when Phil announced his theory about The Dinosaur.

"Why didn't *I* think of that!" Buzz exclaimed. "Sure, he did the job. Criminals are supposed to return to the scene of their crimes. Remember, we saw him watching Mr. Post's store in Kanab. We thought he was watching us!"

"And he returned to the scene of another crime!" Phil said. "He was the one who swiped Mr. Post's fishing tackle box, too. We thought he was spying on us when we saw him at the Fort—but it was Mr. Post he was following!"

"You know," Buzz said in a husky, exhausted voice, "he must have a crazy grudge against Mr. Post and also against anybody Mr. Post is friendly with. That's why he kept bothering us all the time. That's why he tried to steal our Geiger counter."

"That's the answer!" Phil agreed. "We sure ought to report him before he gets away."

"Uh-*uh*!" Buzz protested. "If we squeal on him, he'll say that he saw us prospecting when we weren't supposed to. We have to figure another way to get him caught."

Phil thought he answered Buzz, but he didn't; he had fallen sound asleep. In a second, Buzz had, too.

Phil was dreaming that he was walking along the hot bottom of the Grand Canyon, sweating like anything. Gradually he woke up with a sticky, damp feeling. The sun was beating down on the canvas and making the tent into a suffocating oven. It must be late—very late.

Buzz was still sleeping, dead to the world. There was not a sound outside. The Chief and Aunt Amy and Kitsy must be off somewhere. Groggily Phil pulled himself out of his hot sleeping bag, and as he did so, he felt the Geiger counter near where his head had been. He had better see if the rain had hurt it yesterday; he had been too tired last night. But first he poked his head out of the tent door to make sure no one was around. The station wagon was gone and not a soul could be seen, so he took the machine out and crouched down on the shady side of the tent.

He put the earphones on and flipped the switch. The background count was there, all right. After rubbing it against his T-shirt to take off any moisture that might still cling to the outside of the box, he slowly carried it back into the tent. His movements woke Buzz.

"Hey, dopey, Pop will see you!" Buzz exclaimed.

"He's not around. Nobody is. How are we going to get rid of this doggone machine? We just simply have to find a way of going to Kanab, so we can sell it."

"Maybe Pop will let us take a trip by ourselves again. We wouldn't have to say exactly where we were going. Then we could hitch a ride into Kanab," Buzz suggested. "After we sell the thing back to the man, there won't be any evidence against us. And we can tell Mr. Post that The Dinosaur robbed his store and stole his tackle box!"

But Phil shook his head gloomily. "It sounds fine but it won't work. The Chief will make us rest up today, because we're tired. Then I bet you he'll start running the legs off us again tomorrow morning."

"I'm going to try, anyhow," Buzz decided. "I'm hungry. Did they leave anything around here to eat?"

The boys scrounged in the food boxes and were just sitting down to bread and jam as a starter when the station wagon pulled into camp.

"We went to the post office," Kitsy announced. "I got some letters because *I* wrote some. There was nothing for you boys."

As Phil had feared, the Chief sat down at the table and started laying out plans for the next ten days. Buzz made an effort to get time off for their secret trip to Kanab, but his plea was brushed aside. The three-day delay in his field work had made the Chief more eager than ever to get on with his projects.

Late that afternoon the work started, and it kept on, day after day. They made trips to more bat roosts, some of them a long distance from camp. Then life became really hectic. It was time for old Three-Toes to come back along his travelway again. The Chief wanted to get more pictures of the mountain lion, and the camera had to be set up at the scent station with more catnip bait. On top of that, the Chief was in a state of great excitement because he thought he had located a cave in which only male bats lived. He gave orders right and left and kept the two boys running.

Two or three times Buzz tried to beg a day off, so that he and Phil could hitchhike into Kanab. The Chief was reasonable about refusing. Next week, he said, they could have a holiday. But now he needed help, and the boys had to admit he did. He wasn't just making up work for them.

"It isn't fair to Mr. Post, though," Buzz told Phil remorsefully. "By now The Dinosaur may have escaped for good. He sure hasn't been around here."

This was true. The camp had been peaceful and nothing strange had happened for days.

"I know, but we can't tell anybody anything until we get rid of the Geiger counter, or we'll be in trouble," Phil answered.

Several times the boys had this same discussion, but they could find no solution to their problem. They seemed to grow busier and busier.

One morning they fixed up the scent station. By afternoon they were ready to set off on what might be an overnight trip in search of male bats.

At the last minute Kitsy said, "Daddy, *why* can't I go with you this time? You promised I could help you catch bats sometime. Mommy says she'll take care of Oliver."

"What do you think, Amy?" the Chief asked.

"I think it would be a good idea."

And so the plan was worked out. The Chief would take Phil, Buzz, and Kitsy in the station wagon to the place where the bats roosted. It was a small cave, easy to enter, and they could all help pluck bats off the wall and ceiling. The Chief would band as many as he could; he hoped to get at least several dozen. But this time, instead of letting them loose, he would put them into cages. Then he would return with the cages to camp. His wife would stay in camp and release the bats, after the Chief had had time to return to the cave. This was an experiment to test the bats' homing ability. Camp was twenty miles from the cave, and the Chief expected—or at least he hoped—that the bats would somehow find their way back to their usual roosting place. He planned to go into the cave the next morning, after dawn, and look for specimens that had bands on their wings. If he found any he would know that the male of this type of bat had the ability to fly from an unfamiliar place back to its distant home.

"There's one trouble with the plan," he said. "We've been having rain, and I'd rather try the experiment when the bats don't have any weather problems. A local storm might blow up near the cave this evening. If so we'll just throw our sleeping bags down in the cave entrance where it's dry, and stay there and hope for good weather tomorrow night."

"So I won't expect you till I see you," Aunt Amy said.

"Okay, boys—Phil, you go roll up your sleeping bags," the Chief said briskly. "Buzz, you load that box of food in the station wagon. Kitsy, you put in the bat cages."

As Phil stepped into the tent, dismay suddenly swept over him. "Hey! Buzz, come here!"

The urgency in Phil's voice was real. In spite of the fact that he had the carton of food in his arms, Buzz hurried to the tent. "What's the matter?" he asked.

Phil explained in a low voice, "We forgot about the Geiger counter. It's covered up now with my sleeping bag, but your mother might poke her head in here while we're gone and she'll see it."

Buzz set down the groceries and thought hard. "Put it in the laundry bag," he suggested.

"No, *sir!* She might get energetic and wash our clothes for us while we're gone."

"Hurry up, boys!" the Chief shouted impatiently.

"Oh, heck, let's wrap it up in your sleeping bag and take it with us. We can find some place to hide it when we get to the bat roost," Buzz said.

"Well, then, help me roll it up," Phil said.

Guilt made their fingers fumble, and the Chief was shouting at them again before they had an innocent-looking bundle made.

In a flurry of last-minute orders, the station wagon finally rolled away up the meadow. Phil looked back at the camp and saw Aunt Amy waving and holding Oliver on the leash. For a moment he wondered whether he and Buzz should not have told about their recent experience with The Dinosaur. Aunt Amy was a brave woman, but she was going to be all alone, maybe overnight. What if that queer guy came around and tried to rob the camp? At last Phil put his mind to rest by remembering that there had not been a sign of The Dinosaur, or trouble of any kind, for more than a week. Undoubtedly the guy had gone away.

At Park headquarters they met Boyd Blake who planned to go with them on the expedition, and he followed along behind them in his pickup truck. The dirt road which led from the blacktop down toward the bat cave was the poorest excuse for a road that Phil had ever seen. Recent rain had washed deep ruts in it, and there was a high center with projecting rocks. Several times the station wagon scratched and scraped, and the Chief fumed that the oil pan was probably going to get knocked in.

Finally they reached the end of the road at the rim of the canyon and made the fairly easy hike down to the entrance of the bat roost. Inside the small cave, the collecting and banding went on swiftly. Kitsy was delighted with the ugly, furry little creatures and immediately took charge of the cages in which they were put after they had been banded.

But, in spite of the efficiency with which the Chief worked, it took a long time to catch and band and make the notes on fifty bats—about half of the number they found in the cave. The good weather, Boyd Blake had assured them, was going to stay. Then he had a suggestion to make:

"Look here, Chief," he said, "there's no need for you to knock your car to pieces on that road, making two extra trips tonight. The high center doesn't bother my pickup truck. Let me take the bats to Mrs. Fletcher. You and the kids can stay right here and watch for them to come home."

This proposal pleased everyone, and they all trooped

back up to the end of the road.

"I'm starved," Phil said. "Where's the food box, Buzz? Let's take it out so Kitsy can cook us up a meal." He grinned at her, and she grinned back.

"Well, I *can* cook, dopey, better than you can," she said.

"Food box!" Buzz groaned. "Jumping catfish! Do you know what—"

Phil knew. It was in their tent back at camp—just where Buzz had set it down when they began to solve the problem of stowing the Geiger counter.

Mustering as much self-confidence as he could, Buzz said, "Pop, you got me so rattled, telling us to hurry-hurry-hurry, that do you know what happened? The food box got left in our tent."

The Chief, for once, was speechless.

"We'll just have to go home and have supper, all of us," Kitsy said.

Still silent, the Chief slapped his pants with the flat of his hand and frowned.

"I wish I had something to offer you," Boyd Blake said. "But I haven't a crumb of food in my truck. I'd offer to bring your box to you after I deliver the bats to Mrs. Fletcher, but I can't. I'm all tied up after supper."

Phil watched his uncle, who was obviously making up his mind to something drastic.

Then, quickly, the Chief marched to the station wagon, opened the glove compartment, and looked in. "All right," he announced. "I'm not going to drive over that road any more than I have to. Especially after dark. I have a bar of chocolate here and two of those little boxes of raisins. I'm staying here until morning to see if the bats come back. Buzz, you are staying with me. You can have half the chocolate and half the raisins—for supper *and* breakfast. Phil, you and Kitsy will go back to camp with Boyd, and you'll stay there. You shouldn't have to starve just because Buzz is forgetful."

"Oh, Chief, I don't mind missing a meal or two," Phil protested.

"Well, *I* mind breaking the chocolate up for three," the Chief snapped.

"Come on, Phil," Kitsy said softly. "It's no use arguing with Pop. We might as well go home."

"All right, all aboard the bat wagon," Boyd Blake said.

Silently Phil and Kitsy climbed in beside the Ranger, with the bat cages on the floor of the cab. Buzz looked dismal, as the truck jounced off up the rutted road.

21

"For a guy who likes to eat," Phil thought to himself as they rolled along the blacktop road, "Buzz sure is absent-minded. That's the second time in a week he's had nothing but chocolate because he didn't remember to pick up the grub." Phil had to admit that he himself was partly to blame. But both times the trouble was really caused by the Geiger counter.

"Uh!" he groaned out loud. He had left the Geiger counter in his bedroll in the station wagon! And he had left the bedroll, too. Now what was he going to sleep in?

"What's the matter?" Boyd Blake asked, looking at Phil.

"Nothing—nothing important," Phil answered.

"Doggone the Chief," Phil thought. "He's always in such a hurry he makes you forget things. If he hadn't shooed us off like that, I'd have remembered the sleeping bags." Kitsy's bag was in the station wagon, too, but that wasn't so bad. Her mother could fix her up with coats and stuff, probably.

The sun had gone down, but it was not yet dark, when the pickup neared the turnoff to camp. Another Park Service truck came toward them and a loud honking told Blake that the driver was giving more than a casual greeting. He stopped and so did the other Ranger.

"Mr. Blake! I was hoping I'd run into you. Have you been home yet?"

"No—why?"

"Well, there's a long distance call for you. They said it was urgent. I thought you'd want to know."

"What's it about?"

"I don't know. But whoever it was, they sure did want to get ahold of you."

"Say," Phil broke in, "if it's important, you don't have to take us all the way to camp. We know the shortcut down the hill from here. Kitsy and I can walk and carry the bat cages. They're light."

"Sure, that'll be fun," Kitsy chimed in. "I haven't been to the Rustlers' Fort in a long time."

"Sure you can manage those cages?" Boyd Blake asked.

The little wire containers were very light, even with their load of bats. Phil was already out of the cab door, and Kitsy jumped down after him.

"Be seeing you," Phil called to the Rangers.

"Good luck with the homing bats," Boyd Blake called and drove off.

"Poor Buzz!" Kitsy remarked when they had walked a little way. "He's hungry now, I bet."

"Let's hurry up," Phil said. "I'm hungry *and* thirsty."

"We can get a drink at Rustlers' Fort," Kitsy said.

When they reached the ledge on which the Fort stood, they looked eagerly down at camp. Apparently his aunt was in her tent, but Phil saw that she had built a fire in the fireplace. It gave him a warm, cheerful feeling to see the flames in the evening shadows below.

"Hey, Mommy!" Kitsy yelled in her soft, thin voice.

"She can't hear you from here," Phil said. "All she can hear is the wind shaking the leaves. We'll be there in a few minutes."

"I just wanted her to know I was here so I could wave to her," Kitsy answered.

"I hope she has something ready for us to eat," said Phil.

"She'll be surprised when she finds out that Pop and

Buzz aren't coming home with us," Kitsy said. "We'll eat their share. But we'd better tell her to have lots of breakfast ready for them."

Phil opened the heavy door to the old Fort, and some of the lingering daylight fell across the cement pool where the spring dripped out of the rock. He and Kitsy leaned over, side by side, and started to drink.

A creaking noise behind Phil—then sudden darkness— surprised him. The door had swung shut. He hopped to his feet, groped toward the entrance, and pushed. The wind must have blown it shut. But it didn't budge. He pushed harder.

"Open it up, Phil," Kitsy said. "I can't see."

"I'm trying to. It's stuck." Phil drew back and threw his whole weight against the thick boards.

Then, outside the door, he heard a noise. A rock seemed to be rolling over and over—and somebody seemed to be grunting! The rock crashed against the wood. Somebody had shut them in! Somebody was bracing the door with a big stone!

"Hey! What're you doing? Let us out!" Phil shouted.

"What's the matter?" Kitsy asked.

"Somebody's playing a trick on us," Phil answered.

"Hey! You! This isn't funny! Let us out!"

No sound came from outside except the rolling of another rock.

"Don't be silly!" Kitsy said sensibly. "Who would be playing a trick on us?"

The second rock banged against the door. Phil, thoroughly alarmed, didn't answer Kitsy. His eyes were becoming accustomed to the dark. Thin rays of gray light trickled in through the tiny loopholes that the rustlers had built into the stone wall for their guns, long ago. Quickly he moved over and peered out of one hole that opened on the side where the door was. He was sure he saw the form of a man disappearing in the dusk at the end of the ledge.

"Phil, what's the matter?" Kitsy said, and her voice was shaky. "Open the door."

"Look, Kitsy, I've been trying. But somebody piled rocks against it. Somebody's up to something, but I don't know what. Just keep quiet and I'll try again."

Actually, Phil did know what must have happened. Somebody who was hiding near the ledge had seen them enter the Fort. He had closed the door quietly, then pushed the slide-bolt into position. After that the rocks were added, to make sure that Phil and Kitsy couldn't get out. But why?

What was it all about? Who had done it?

The Dinosaur—of that Phil had no doubt. The Dinosaur knew about this place; this was where Phil and Buzz had seen him first. He had followed them around, even down into the Canyon. Maybe he had followed them ever since and they didn't know about it. But what was the big idea?

"I want to get out of here!" Kitsy said as if it were a simple, practical problem to solve and Phil was not solving it.

"Kitsy," Phil said, "somebody has locked us in. It's no joke, and I can't do anything about it right now. Just let me think."

"Mommy will let us out. Yell to her," Kitsy suggested.

Phil started to put his mouth to one of the loopholes. Then he stopped. What would happen if Aunt Amy should hear and come up the hill?

"No, Kitsy," he said. "I don't want to yell. The guy out there is The Dinosaur. He might bop her on the head or something if she came running up here. Say, I bet that's why he locked us in. He *wants* her to come looking for us, so he can have a chance to rob the whole camp!"

"But I don't want to stay here!" Kitsy began to whimper. "I don't like it here. It's dark."

She was right. The last rays of sunlight had disappeared. By looking through a loophole, Phil could see that it was not yet totally dark outside, but inside he could scarcely see Kitsy. He still had his flashlight in his jacket pocket. Now he turned it on and studied the walls and looked for anything he could use as a tool to break out of the Fort. The stone walls seemed a foot thick, and the stones were tightly laid, one on the other. There wasn't even a stick that Phil could use. The Rangers had cleaned this place out completely when they fixed it as a water-supply shed. Phil searched his pockets, but he knew already that he had left his knife in the jeans he had worn yesterday.

He and Kitsy were trapped.

Phil tried to keep calm, and to think. No one would start looking for them until tomorrow. Aunt Amy was not expecting them necessarily, so she wouldn't come looking. Boyd Blake had every reason to suppose they had just walked the short distance down to camp. He wouldn't think of checking up on them. The Chief would wait at the bat cave until the little night-fliers all returned. Then he would spend a long time looking for any one of them that might have a band on it. Naturally, he wouldn't find any, because Phil and Kitsy had the banded bats locked up in the Fort. It would certainly be the middle of the morning before the Chief would give up and decide that his experiment was a complete failure. Then, after he got back to camp and found that Phil and Kitsy had never returned, he would have to look for Boyd Blake, and that would take more time. But suppose something happened to Aunt Amy and the camp during the night? Phil knew he *had* to think of some way to tell somebody what was going on.

"Phil, what if nobody comes and gets us?" Kitsy asked.

"Oh, they will, Kitsy. Your father will come tomorrow morning."

"You mean—we have to stay here all *night?*"

"It looks that way."

"I'm scared—I'm cold—I don't want to stay here."

Phil flashed the beam of light all around the little room, looking for a comfortable spot on which to sit or lie.

As the light fell on the cages, Kitsy said with a tremble in her voice, "Look at them. Even the bats want to get out."

The little animals were stirring, creeping around over the wire of the cage sides, trying to find some way to start their night flight.

"They're hungry, too," Kitsy remarked.

"Hey!" Phil exclaimed. "I bet we could let them out.

They're small enough to go through those loopholes. We could pick them out of the cages one at a time and stick them into the holes—then they could fly away all right."

"Okay," Kitsy agreed. "Shall we do it now?"

"We might as well."

As Phil reached into the cage and grasped the first silky body, an inspiration struck him. He put the bat back.

"Kitsy! If the Chief's experiment works, these bats will fly right back to where he is. If we can just put a message on them, he'll get it and come and let us out!"

"How could we put a message on a bat?" Kitsy asked.

"Maybe we could write something on the bands."

"Oh, the bands are too tiny. You can hardly see the numbers that are stamped on them."

Phil knew she was right. The little pieces of metal were less than a quarter inch long and an eighth inch wide.

"I know!" Kitsy said. "Let's write messages on a piece of paper and fasten them to the bats' wings with the bands!"

"It won't work," Phil said, discouraged. "The bats would chew the paper off. The Chief said they even try to chew the bands off when they're put on too tight. We have to think of something else."

"Besides, we haven't got any paper and pencil, have we?"

"I don't know. Let me see—I have the pencil I was using when I made notes about bats in the Chief's notebook. But he has the notebook."

A search of all his pockets produced no paper. Then he took out his wallet. He knew there wasn't any money in it, but there might just be some kind of paper that he had forgotten. No—nothing but a couple of thick cards and the book of postage stamps that he was supposed to use on the postcards he never got around to sending.

Stamps! He had it!

"Kitsy! We can stick postage stamps on the bats! The stamps are bright. Your father will be sure to see them when the bats get to the cave. The glue will stick to their fur!"

"Do you think it'll work?" Kitsy asked, greatly excited.

"We have to try. If we stick the stamps on their backs they can't chew them off."

"But a stamp is too little to write on."

"I don't know. I can write pretty small. Hold the flashlight for me."

Quickly Phil rubbed the pencil lead on the rock wall to sharpen its point. He thought a moment, then wrote, *"Help! Locked in Rustlers' Fort, Phil."*

"See, Kitsy, you can say a lot on a stamp."

"Write my name on some of 'em, I'm locked up here, too. Make it good and black." She began to sound almost as if she were having fun.

Kitsy held the light and watched Phil write for a few moments. Then she asked, "Can you write 'hurry' on some of them, too?"

"Don't have to," Phil answered. "When your Pop sees the stamps, he'll hurry all right."

It took quite a while to put the messages on all twenty-four stamps in Phil's book. It took even longer to stick the stamps securely on the backs of the fluttering little creatures. After Phil was sure the stamp wouldn't come off, he lifted each bat up into a loophole, and soon it disappeared into the outer air.

When the job was done, the flashlight was nearly worn out. Phil couldn't guess how long they had been locked in the Fort, but it might have been two hours or more.

"Now," Kitsy said with a tired sigh, "let's turn the others loose."

When that was finished, there was nothing to do but huddle close together in a corner and wait. In spite of the discomfort of the chilly night air and the hard rocks, first Kitsy then Phil dropped off to sleep.

22 STRANGE RESCUE

"Why don't they *come?*" Kitsy said for the hundredth time.

The bit of sky that Phil could see through the loopholes had been light for what seemed like a couple of hours.

"Kitsy, don't get impatient. We just have to wait."

There was a long silence, and then Kitsy asked, "Are you very hungry?"

Phil didn't answer. He heard something outside the Fort. Footsteps!

"Chief!" he yelled.

There was a clatter on the bare rock surface of the ledge. And through the loophole he caught a glimpse of Lulubelle who had apparently come to have a drink of water at the overflow of the spring.

Phil felt disappointment, but he was somehow also

reassured. It was good to have something familiar turn up, even if it was only Lulubelle.

In the dim room he and Kitsy shifted from one loop-hole to another, hoping to see somebody. Now and again Phil shouted through one of the holes, "Help! We're here!" But there was no conviction in his calls, and his voice was growing hoarse.

At last a beam of direct sunlight began to pour through the loophole near the door. It must be about seven o'clock, Phil calculated. If any bats with stamps on their backs had returned to their roost, and if the Chief had seen them, he ought to be along any minute.

Phil's guess was a shrewd one. Before long he could hear voices that seemed to be coming from the direction of the blacktop road.

"Kitsy! Phil!" The voices sounded closer.

Desperately Phil and Kitsy shouted back.

In a moment Buzz and the Chief rushed onto the ledge.

"Get us out!" Kitsy wailed.

"What happened?" Buzz called.

"Never mind what happened," the Chief said. "Help me roll these rocks away."

When the door swung open, Kitsy rushed out into her

father's arms. He hugged her, and then flung an arm around Phil. "Are you all right?"

"I guess so, except I'm—I'm scared," Kitsy blurted out. Now, for the first time, she burst into tears.

"Is Aunt Amy all right?" Phil asked. "I was afraid the guy who locked us up might have bothered her, too."

"Amy!" The Chief looked frightened. "We haven't been back to camp yet! Who was it? Who locked you in here?" Already the Chief had started down the trail toward camp.

"It must have been The Dinosaur," Phil said, hurrying after him.

"How do you know?" the Chief called back over his shoulder.

"He's followed us everywhere. He even followed Buzz and me down to Phantom Ranch."

The Chief said nothing more. He was breathless from running when he reached camp. "Amy!" he shouted. "Are you all right?"

His wife came out of the wall tent. "Of course I am. What's wrong with *you*?"

Kitsy, who had been dry-eyed as long as they were hurrying down the hill, rushed to her mother and began to sob.

"Kitsy, dear, what is it?"

Everybody began to talk at once, but out of it all the story began to emerge.

"Why didn't you boys tell me that the man you call The Dinosaur followed you down into the Canyon?" the Chief asked after a while. There was no anger, only worry, in his voice.

"Oh, we—we didn't want to upset you," Buzz fumbled.

"Anyway, we found out that he is a thief or crazy or something," Phil said. "Are you sure he didn't steal something from camp last night?"

Aunt Amy looked at Phil thoughtfully. "I'm sure nothing has been bothered. But maybe I know the reason why. I was reading a book until very late. And then I fell asleep with the light on. If anybody was around, he would have thought I was still awake. And this morning I got up about dawn and made some recordings of bird songs, right here by the tents."

By now Buzz had opened the food locker which was attached to a tree. He took out a loaf of bread and some butter. "In case you want to know, Ma, I did it again. I forgot the food yesterday. The Chief and I didn't have anything but a little chocolate and raisins to eat."

"All Phil and I had was nothing!" Kitsy said.

As the Chief bolted his breakfast, he quizzed Phil, Kitsy, and Buzz, trying to figure out what had happened and why. Shamefacedly, he admitted he had thought that the postage stamps on the bats might possibly have been a practical joke that Phil had thought up. Now he intended to go to headquarters as fast as he could and ask the Rangers to look for the madman who was at large. The person who locked up Phil and Kitsy must be insane.

Everybody began talking at once, and finally Aunt Amy took command. "There's no need to get hysterical," she said. "Children, I think you all ought to go and lie down and rest. You're exhausted. Herbert and I have to talk quietly for a while and decide exactly what to do."

"I *have* decided what to do," the Chief said excitedly. "We're going to see Boyd Blake immediately."

"We don't have to go this minute. I think we ought to move out of here. But I want to discuss it calmly."

"All right. As soon as I go and get the station wagon, you'll have a rest, kids," the Chief ordered.

In a few minutes he was back. The boys took their sleeping bags out of the station wagon. Kitsy carried hers under one arm and Oliver under the other and staggered into the wall tent. Phil and Buzz rolled out their bags in their tent, and in Phil's was that blasted Geiger counter.

"If it isn't one thing it's another. What are we going to do with this white elephant?"

Phil wearily pushed the Geiger counter off onto the floor between himself and Buzz, then lay back on his sleeping bag, glad to relax on something halfway soft.

Buzz idly began to fiddle with the counter.

"I sure hate to get rid of this," he said. "Say, maybe my folks will decide to move our camp somewhere outside the Park, where it's legal to prospect."

"Aw, we're not twenty-one years old," Phil groaned with his eyes closed.

"I bet there's some way," Buzz said and put the earphones on. He turned the switch.

Phil shifted and sleepily opened his eyes. He glanced at his cousin, and the look on Buzz's face was a dead giveaway that something had excited him. Buzz scrambled to his hands and knees and began crawling all around the tent, holding the Geiger counter.

Phil reached over and pulled the earphones off Buzz. "Are you crazy with the heat?" he whispered.

"Put 'em on yourself," Buzz whispered back. "We've got uranium right smack under the middle of our tent!"

Phil went through the same procedure Buzz had followed. Sure enough, a rapid clicking filled his ears when he held the Geiger counter near the floor beside the center pole of the tent. The count decreased as the small box was moved away in any direction from this particular point.

"Well, what do you know!" Phil exclaimed.

"Jiggers! We better hide this thing quick!" Buzz exclaimed. "That's Boyd Blake's voice out there. If he finds we have a Geiger counter, we'll sure be in trouble. He's a nice guy, but he works for the Park and he'd turn us in."

Phil quickly stuffed the counter under the head of his sleeping bag, and the two boys emerged from the tent. The Chief had just about finished telling the Ranger that Phil and Kitsy had been prisoners in the Rustlers' Fort.

"What an ordeal the kids must have gone through! I *never* should have let them start home alone!" Boyd Blake exclaimed.

"Nobody blames you, Boyd," the Chief replied. "The main thing now is to catch the monster who locked the children up last night."

"You're right, but I'm afraid I have to pile more bad news on you," the Ranger said. "I came to see you about an entirely different problem. It has me very much worried.

I suppose Phil told you the reason why I dumped him and Kitsy on the road last night. I was stopped by a message that I had a long-distance telephone call. I went back to my office and tried to put the call through, but I didn't succeed until just a little while ago, and here I am. Have you seen that mountain lion?"

"No," the Chief said a little impatiently.

"Well, he's due back on his regular circuit just about today. My telephone call had to do with him. Remember you told me about the boxer dog he killed? Well, I finally got around to writing to the folks who lost the dog and I told them your story. They just found out yesterday that there was an epidemic of rabies in the dogs in their town. Their boxer had been in a fight and was bitten. Now, you know, Chief, how infected dogs behave. In one stage they run away from their masters, just the way this boxer did. Later they sometimes go crazy and will attack anything. From what you told me, I suspect that the boxer actually attacked the lion."

"Great Scott!" the Chief cried. "You mean the lion probably has rabies." He stopped and calculated for a minute. "And just about now he'll be in the furious phase of the disease!"

"That's exactly what I mean," Boyd Blake said.

"I thought lions didn't attack people, Chief," Phil said.

"They don't unless—" the Chief's face was very serious.

"That's right. There are several cases on record when lions with rabies attacked human beings. I've sent some fellows out along his travelway to try to shoot him. Meantime you people must get out of here. Sorry to spoil your expedition, but it won't be safe for you to come back here until we're sure there aren't any infected animals around."

"I don't ever want to come back," Kitsy said. "I don't want to be where anybody can lock me up all night again."

"All the more reason for leaving this place," Boyd Blake said. "I'll get word as fast as I can to the Park Superintendent. He will have some men sent out to look for whoever pulled that trick. It must be somebody who's off his rocker. But we'll have to find him, anyway."

"A mad dog, a mad lion, a madman—the whole thing's insane," the Chief fumed. "Boys, pull your tent down."

Phil and Buzz moved stuff out through the door of the tent, taking care first to wrap the Geiger counter once more in a sleeping bag.

"You know, Buzz," Phil said regretfully, "we'll probably never be allowed to come back here. I wish we could have a sample of that uranium under our tent."

"Maybe we can if we work fast," Buzz said. "Go get the trenching shovel. It's over by the fireplace."

When the tent was down, and before they started to roll it up, Buzz started quickly to work, glancing every once in a while in his father's direction. The earth under the center of the tent was soft. A few strokes of the shovel and Buzz struck something hard.

"I've hit the rock already," he said triumphantly to Phil.

Phil peered down as Buzz scraped earth away in a frenzy. A few additional strokes of the small shovel revealed something dark green.

"It's a box!" Phil exclaimed.

Now both of them dug with their hands in the soft earth. It was a fishing tackle box.

"That's probably the one Mr. Post lost!" Phil said in wonder, pulling it out of the hole. He pushed the catch.

"Holy mackerel!" Buzz whispered.

The box was full of shining objects—bracelets, rings—diamond rings—beautiful wrist watches, dozens of them!

"Chief! Everybody, come over here quick!" Phil yelled.

"Will you kids pay attention to business!" his uncle called back angrily. "We have to hurry and get out of here."

Impetuously Buzz picked up the box and strode toward his father. "We're not wasting time. Look at this." He slammed the open box down on the camp table.

The three adults and Kitsy stared at it in astonishment.

"What's that stuff?" Kitsy said first.

"Jewelry and watches, dopey," Buzz answered.

"It must be the stuff that was stolen from Mr. Post's store," Phil explained. "And it's in a fishing tackle box—which he said he'd lost."

"How did you find it?" Kitsy asked.

"Dug it up," Buzz answered.

"But where—" Aunt Amy asked, puzzled.

"Right under our tent. It must have been there all the time," Buzz answered.

"But why—" Aunt Amy was still puzzled.

Phil had been thinking hard. How, in fact, had they discovered the box? Suddenly he had it. "See the radium dials on some of those watches?" he shouted. "That's what did it. That's what our Geiger counter picked up!"

"Your *what!*" the Chief snorted.

The secret was out, but it was too late to do anything about it. Maybe the discovery of the box would balance off against the Geiger counter they weren't supposed to have.

Order finally began to come out of the excitement and chaos. The tents were down, and everything had been packed into the station wagon and trailer. The fishing tackle box, with its amazing contents, was to be taken to the Park Superintendent, who would notify the authorities in Kanab.

"Whew!" Buzz said to Phil, taking his first moment of rest. "You know how the loot got under our tent, don't you? The Dinosaur buried it there. Remember the day when Mom and Kitsy came back and found our tent caved in—and the footprints?"

"Those were the garbage collector's footprints," Phil reminded him.

"We never asked him, did we?" Buzz said. "No, sir. He only said he'd seen a mess that Lulubelle made. She just probably kicked the garbage pail over. Don't you see? The Dinosaur buried the loot and then ran into the woods."

"But why did he do it?" Phil asked.

"Because he's nuts, and he wanted to put the blame on us!" Buzz said. "Don't you see? He swiped Mr. Post's tackle box. Then he put the jewelry in it, and then he buried it. He's so nutty he didn't even want the jewels!"

Phil started to digest this plausible theory, but the Chief interrupted.

"Now, you boys police the camp and make sure we haven't left anything," he said.

Phil looked all over the area in which they had been living. It was remarkably neat, considering the hullabaloo of packing in a hurry. One thing which he had not noticed before caught his eye. Leaning against the side of Boyd Blake's pickup truck were two high-powered rifles.

"Say, where did those come from?" he called out.

"I brought 'em," Blake answered. "If so many things hadn't been happening around here, I'd have said something about them before. I told you some Rangers are hunting for the lion. I was going to start out on the trail from here, and I thought maybe the Chief would join me."

"Me?" the Chief said, startled. "I'm no good with a gun.

Don't know what's wrong with my aim, but I've never been able to hit the broad side of a barn."

"Could I go?" Phil asked eagerly. "I'm on the high school rifle team."

Boyd Blake turned and looked questioningly at the Chief.

"He's right, Boyd. He's a real marksman," the Chief said.

"How would you feel if I took him along? This is dangerous business, you know," the Ranger said.

"Phil's got good sense," his uncle answered. "Are you sure you want to go, Phil?"

Phil was so choked up with excitement that he could scarcely speak. "Could I go? Oh, boy!"

"Chief, I want to go, too," Buzz put in.

"Sorry, I've got only two guns, and I couldn't let anyone come along who was unarmed," Boyd Blake said.

"I suppose you're right," Buzz mumbled regretfully. "I'm not much of a shot, anyway."

Phil picked up the rifle and looked at it in admiration. It was a beautiful, high-powered repeater.

"Are you familiar with this type?" the Ranger asked.

"Sure." There wasn't a thing he needed to be told.

Kitsy's job, during the hurly-burly, had been to keep Oliver out of the way. Now she sat on a rock off to one side with the enormous kitten flopped across her lap. To amuse herself she had been watching birds through her mother's field glasses.

"Come, Kitsy," Aunt Amy said. "We're ready to go."

Kitsy lugged Oliver to the station wagon and climbed in. "Here's your field glasses, Mommy," she said. "Do you know what? I just saw Mr. Post through them. He's in the woods over there on the other side of the meadow. Want me to go tell him we found his fishing box?"

"Are you *sure* you saw him?" the Chief asked.

"Of course I did. I wouldn't say I did if I hadn't," Kitsy answered.

Her parents knew this was true.

"Boyd," the Chief said, "Kitsy saw Post over there, undoubtedly going on another fishing trip down Dry Bones Canyon. Somebody better head him off. The trail he takes follows the lion's travelway!"

With horror, Phil saw a picture in his mind. A rabid beast was leaping on the unsuspecting fisherman. Tensely he grabbed the rifle and called over his shoulder, "Hurry up. The scent station is at the top of the hill. The lion may be right there!"

"By George, he's right," the Chief cried.

Without more words, Phil and the Ranger strode off across the meadow as fast as they could walk. Near the opposite side, Phil called, "Mr. Post! Stop!"

The two of them paused a moment to hear any reply. But the sound that came to them was that of feet pounding up the hill. They called again. The man surely heard— now why was he running away? As Phil lunged up the hill he tried to make sense of the man's behavior. Mr. Post must have seen them coming. He must have seen their guns. He was frightened! That was the answer. But he wouldn't be afraid unless he had done something that was wrong. What could he have done that was wrong?

Was—was Mr. Post the one who had locked Phil and Kitsy up last night?

Panting hard, Phil struggled to maintain his pace. Thoughts kept tumbling over each other in his head as fast as his feet struck the ground. Then suddenly one idea acted like a magnet and drew all the loose parts of his thoughts together.

Mr. Post had robbed his own store and had buried the loot under his own tent!

Buzz was all wrong when he said The Dinosaur had buried the loot. Post had put it there! That explained why he had been so angry the day the Fletcher party came into his camp. That explained why he had been so angry at Phil and Buzz when they took down his tent. The jewelry was buried, and he couldn't dig it up with an audience.

All this time, Post had pretended to be friendly, hoping to find out a time when they wouldn't be in camp. But somebody was almost always there. So at last he had got desperate. That was why he locked up Phil and Kitsy in the Rustlers' Fort. He had expected that Aunt Amy would go and look for them. Then, as soon as she left camp, he planned to dig the box up.

With renewed energy, Phil trotted along the path which leveled off at the saddle in the ridge. Fifty yards ahead lay the scent station.

Post, thought Phil, had probably been hovering around the meadow all morning, just waiting for them to leave. Now he was running away because he thought his crime had been discovered. He was hoping to escape into Dry Bones Canyon where he always fished and where he could hide. But, criminal or not, he had to be warned about the rabid lion!

Phil had been trotting along in front of Boyd Blake. He stopped to wait and to listen for the pounding feet ahead.

But there was no sound except for his own heavy breathing and that of the Ranger who caught up with him in a moment or two.

"He's disappeared," Phil gasped.

"That crazy idiot! Why doesn't he stop? Post! Hey! Post! Stop!"

There was no answer.

Phil started to tell the Ranger his theory of why Post was running away, but Boyd Blake said, "Sh! I want to listen." He heard nothing. "Where's that scent station?" he demanded nervously.

"Just ahead. We'll see it in a minute."

"All right. You stay behind me. Keep your eyes peeled."

Moving cautiously now, for fear the lion might be attracted by the catnip close by, they walked down the travelway.

"Boyd!" Phil suddenly whispered. "Look! By that big rock!"

A flick of motion had caught his eye, but now he saw nothing. "I thought something moved—"

"All right. I'll go to the right. You go to the left."

Stealthily they began a wide circuit of the rock with their guns held poised.

Dry branches snapped, and Post burst from behind the rock.

"Danger! Mountain lion!" Boyd Blake yelled.

But Post dashed on. He leaped out in the small clearing, at the other end of which was the scent station. Even as he ran, he glanced at the spot on the tree where the catnip sandwich had been placed, then froze in his tracks.

Wildly biting at the tree was the mountain lion.

The sound of feet diverted the lion from its attack on the scented tree. It turned. Then—unlike a cat—it charged the man. One great bound closed nearly half the distance between it and Post.

Phil's rifle was at his shoulder and he fired, just as the lion launched into a second great, furious bound. An instant later, Boyd Blake's rifle went off. The huge, tawny animal lay kicking spasmodically in the gravel. Only a few feet separated Post from the concentrated bundle of death that had launched itself at him.

Complete and utter panic overcame Post. Like a candle near a hot stove, he sagged over and collapsed.

Boyd Blake ran forward and fired a final precautionary shot into the lion's head. Then he stood, tense and pale, over the man who still lay panting on the ground.

Phil was at his side in an instant with his rifle pointed directly at Post.

"Wheoof! That was a close one! Beautiful shot, Phil. You saved this guy's life," Boyd Blake said.

Phil realized that his rifle was wavering. His hands shook with excitement. But he held it resolutely pointing at Post.

"You can take it easy now," Boyd Blake said. "Sit down and have a rest."

"You better search him, Boyd, to see if he's got a gun," Phil muttered breathlessly.

"Snap out of it!" The Ranger's voice showed annoyance. He moved toward Phil to take the rifle away.

"Don't! Stay back and I'll tell you something," Phil said.

Alarmed, Boyd Blake drew back and looked in blank amazement at the tense, strained figure. Phil was plainly dead serious.

"This guy locked Kitsy and me up last night. He's a crook, and that's why he was running away from us," Phil said slowly and distinctly.

Post started to pull himself up into a sitting position. Then he put one arm in front of his eyes, sagged forward, and began to sob like a great big baby.

24

Phil continued to stand, pale and alert, with the rifle pointed at the big man who was a shapeless sobbing heap on the ground. He had told Boyd Blake once, and then all over again, the reasons why he was sure Post had robbed his own store, buried the loot under the tent, and tried for more than three weeks to recover it.

The Ranger looked confused and uncertain. He seemed to be trying to make up his mind what to do. His eyes went from Post to Phil to the lion stretched out on the ground.

"Boyd, we have to get this guy out of here," Phil said. "Come on, Mr. Post. Stand up."

The Ranger put down his rifle and started to help the big man to his feet.

Phil was suddenly alarmed. "Don't touch him! He might try something!" he exclaimed.

Slowly, clumsily, Post got to his feet.

"You go ahead of us down the hill," Phil said to him.

"All right, Mr. Post, start walking," Boyd Blake said, picking up the rifle. "I'm sorry to have to do this, but if we've made a mistake it can be straightened out later."

Post was a picture of exhaustion and dejection. He stumbled down the hill with Phil and the Ranger walking side by side behind him, their rifles at their sides.

By the time they reached the edge of the meadow, however, the big man was beginning to pull himself together. He turned slowly and faced his captors.

"Look here," he said with some firmness in his voice, "you can get into a lot of trouble for chasing me and threatening me. If you let me go now, I won't have you arrested. I'm surprised at you, Mr. Blake, for letting a kid get you mixed up in a thing like this."

Before the Ranger could answer, a shout came from the woods below the Rustlers' Fort, and Buzz, running at top speed, burst into the meadow. He was so excited, obviously, that he paid no attention to the fact that Phil and the Ranger were facing Post with their rifles pointed.

"Quick! Come up to the Fort!" he yelled. "We caught The Dinosaur! Pop's guarding him!"

Phil looked at Buzz. "What? Why?"

"Dinosaur!" Boyd Blake said, puzzled. "What are you talking about?"

"The crook! The guy that robbed Mr. Post—that crazy man—we got him locked up. Don't just stand there!"

"Come here, Buzz," Phil said. "Calm down and listen to me a minute. The Dinosaur isn't the crook, the way you thought he was. Mr. Post robbed his own store—"

"Don't say that again, you young idiot!" Post shouted.

For the first time Buzz realized who the fourth member of the party was. "Oh, hello, Mr. Post," he said. "Phil, what are you talking about?"

With his face serious, and his rifle pointed, Phil answered, "Listen to me, Buzz. And, Mr. Post, don't you interrupt. This guy robbed his own store. How do you think the stuff got under our tent, if he didn't put it there?"

"That's enough, Phil." Boyd Blake was the one who interrupted. "Buzz, what's this about your father locking somebody up?"

"Don't just *stand* there," Buzz pleaded. "You have to come up to the Fort. I'll tell you on the way."

"All right," Boyd Blake said. "We'll have to go and see what this is about. Mr. Post, you lead the way."

The big man looked at Phil's rifle, shrugged, and turned toward the trail. Boyd Blake started out behind him.

"Walk beside me, Buzz," Phil ordered. "Now tell me what happened."

Buzz was completely amazed by the performance, but he fell into line and began to talk.

"Pop was just driving out of the meadow when I turned around and took a last look up at the Rustlers' Fort. I thought I saw somebody standing there on the ledge. I kept watching and got a good look. It was The Dinosaur."

"Buzz, who is this Dinosaur?" Boyd Blake asked.

Buzz explained, then went on, "I made Pop agree to stop the station wagon on the blacktop so he and I could go down to the ledge and keep an eye on him until Mom could find some Rangers to arrest him. We sneaked down the shortcut, and there he was, on the far end of the ledge. I was afraid he might have a gun, but we couldn't see any on him. In a little while he got thirsty and went into the Fort. Boy, you should have seen me! I ran up and slammed that door and bolted it, before the Chief knew what was going on. Then I rolled the two big rocks against the door, just the way he did when he locked you and Kitsy in!"

"He didn't lock us in," Phil announced. "Mr. Post, stop!

If The Dinosaur has a gun, he can shoot us through the loophole by the door. If he's as crazy as we think he is, he might do it!"

"He can't do it. I fixed that." Buzz chuckled. "I stuffed a rock in that loophole and then I leaned a log against it."

"Okay. Let's go," Boyd Blake said.

When they came in sight of the Fort, Phil beheld a strange spectacle. There was the Chief, standing beside the door of the Fort with a large stick clutched in his hand. He was not going to let his prisoner escape.

"Let me out of here!" a muffled voice came from inside.

"Here we are, Chief," Buzz called cheerfully.

The Chief whirled around. "Boyd, will you take charge of this lunatic in here?" He dropped his stick and began to move toward the party. "Mr. Post, we've caught the character who's been causing us so much trouble."

"Chief, don't come any closer," Phil warned him. "Mr. Post is the criminal."

"What are you talking about?" the Chief snapped.

Immediately, Post saw his advantage. "Mr. Fletcher, I don't know what has got into these two, but I wish you would straighten them out. They have been threatening me with their guns, and I've had about enough of it."

"Chief, there is a lot here I don't understand," Boyd Blake said quickly. "I don't know who's right and who's wrong, but until I find out, I'm not taking any chances."

"Let me out!" came another bellow from the Fort.

"You, in there!" Boyd Blake called out. "Keep quiet. I'm a Park Service Ranger. Mr. Fletcher seems to think you have committed some serious crimes. I don't know. I still want to hear the whole story. I have somebody else out here who is accused of the same crimes. I'll open the door when I make up my mind whether to arrest one or both of you."

"Phil!" the Chief said. "Put that gun down. I wish you would, too, Boyd. You make me nervous."

From inside the Fort came the question: "Ranger! Who have you got out there?"

"A man by the name of Post—" Boyd Blake began.

"Listen to me!" came the voice again. "That man robbed his own jewelry store in Kanab."

Suddenly, Post looked like a balloon that had been punctured. He sank down on one of the rocks.

"How do you know?" Boyd Blake shouted.

"I'm a detective—an insurance company detective. We've known all along that Post did the job. Now please let me out of here!" the voice wailed.

Boyd Blake considered. "How do you know?"

"I have absolute proof. That dope faked the breaking of the lock on his front door. All the jimmying was done from *inside* the store. We could tell by the way the holes were bored around the lock."

"What do you have to say, Mr. Post?" Boyd Blake asked.

Post only shook his head and kept his eyes on the ground.

"Hey, you!" Buzz shouted suddenly. "I don't believe you. You tried to rob Phil and me at Phantom Ranch!"

The Ranger, who had made a move as if to release the prisoner, turned and said sharply, "What's this?"

"That's right, Boyd," Phil said quickly. "He did follow us down into the Canyon, and he searched our knapsacks."

"Listen to me!" The voice inside the Fort was squeaking by now. "If you'll let me out, I'll explain."

"You can explain it all right from where you are."

"I did go to Phantom Ranch, and for a very good reason," the voice shouted indignantly. "These Fletchers were so friendly with Post, and I trailed him back here so many times, that it looked as if the Fletchers were in on the deal. I had to explore every angle. I thought maybe Post had left the jewelry with them, and those two kids were trying to run it out across the bridge at the bottom of the Canyon.

I went through their packs to see if they had the stuff! All they had was a Geiger counter. Now will you let me out?"

For one moment, Phil took his eyes off Post and glanced at Buzz who looked as troubled as he felt. Now they were in for it. The Dinosaur had squealed on them.

But the Ranger called to the prisoner: "You haven't told me why this man would want to rob his own store."

"How long do I have to stay here answering your stupid questions? It's obvious. He wanted to collect the insurance. That's why I'm on the job. The guy doesn't like to work; all he wants to do is go fishing. He thought he had a smart way to make ten thousand dollars, so he could just take it easy and fish whenever he felt like it and have a good time schmoozing around with people. He's a dope, I tell you."

Right then Phil had a brilliant idea. "You, in there!" he yelled. "Where were you just before dark last night?"

"What's that got to do with things? Let me out of here!"

"It's got a lot to do with this mess," Phil answered.

"Well, I was talking to a lady named Mrs. Blake. Her husband is some kind of Ranger. I was trying to find Post. He gave me the slip when he left Kanab yesterday, and I thought maybe Blake could tell me whether Post had come to the Park as I suspected he had. I waited till way after dark, but he still didn't come home. Mrs. Blake knows I talked to her and then waited for a long time in front of her cabin. Now will you let me out?"

Phil, who had been looking at Post all this time, glanced at the Ranger. Boyd Blake's face told him all he needed to know. The prisoner in the Fort was speaking the truth.

"All right, Post, you did it!" Phil said. "You locked Kitsy and me in the Fort last night. You were waiting up here, hoping my aunt would go away for some reason. Then you heard Kitsy and me talking. You thought Aunt Amy would come looking for us, if we didn't turn up for supper. You waited and waited. But her light was on almost all night. You thought she was awake and you didn't dare to try and dig up your fishing tackle box."

"Hey!" Buzz interrupted. "He was the one that knocked over our tent that time! We thought it was Lulubelle or the garbage man who made the footprints."

He paused, and Phil went on. "Buzz is right, Post. You sent that phony letter, too. You thought that would make us all leave camp and go to Boyd Blake's office. And you tried to make it seem like nothing but a crazy joke by sticking letters in a lot of people's cars—"

Buzz interrupted again: "I bet you even loosened a wire

on the ignition in your car or something, so that your wife was stuck that day. You were hoping she would ask Mom to go and help. That would have given you a chance to dig up the loot."

"You're right!" yelled the prisoner inside the Fort. "I was a dope. I searched your camp that day. I was there, and so Post couldn't get in. Let me out of here!"

Phil had another idea. "Post, you were the guy who dug the holes in the road, so our car or somebody else's car would get stuck. You hoped *that* would make everybody leave camp."

Boyd Blake had been looking more and more mystified. But for the third time he said to Post: "What have you got to say? Is all this true?"

Wearily, the big man nodded his head.

Phil stared at Post, who seemed utterly crushed, and in a way Phil felt sorry for the man. He, Phil McKenney, was more grown-up than this miserable fellow.

Simultaneously two voices spoke up. "Let me out of here!" came from inside the Fort. And the Chief rapped out, "I heard three shots, Boyd. Did you kill the lion?"

Boyd Blake nodded. And Post said in a choked voice, "That boy saved my life."

"Is that true, Boyd?" the Chief asked.

The Ranger nodded again.

"Boyd," Buzz said, "Phil and I didn't know it was against the law to have a Geiger counter in the Park."

The Ranger looked confused for the nth time today. "I don't get you. It's *not* against the law."

"But the fellow told us it was—"

"I don't know who gave you that idea. The Park isn't open for mining, if that's what you mean. But a Geiger counter can't hurt anything. If you find radioactivity let me know. The point is that the Park is to be kept in its natural beauty, not spoiled by mines. There's plenty of uranium *outside* the Park. Isn't that true, Chief?"

The Chief slowly began to grin. He looked first at Buzz, then at Phil. "*Anybody,*" he said with emphasis, "who told you not to use a Geiger counter is a dope!"

"Clickety-clickety-click!" Buzz said.

"Click-click!" said Phil.

"Checkety-checkety-check!" the Chief added with a twinkle in his eye.

"Let me out of here!" roared the voice from the Fort.

"Double-check!" the Chief said. And as Post moved to one side, he and Phil rolled the rocks away from the door.

Whitman
CLASSICS

Five Little Peppers Midway

Mrs. Wiggs of the
Cabbage Patch

Fifty Famous Fairy Tales

Eight Cousins

Little Women

Black Beauty

Five Little Peppers and
How They Grew

Treasure Island

Heidi

The Call of the Wild

Tom Sawyer

Beautiful Joe

Adventures of Sherlock Holmes

Little Lame Prince

Here are some of the best-loved stories of all time.
Delightful...intriguing...never-to-be-forgotten
tales that you will read again and again. Start
your own home library of WHITMAN CLASSICS
so that you'll always have exciting books at your
finger tips.

Whitman

REG. U.S. PAT. OFF.

Whitman ADVENTURE and MYSTERY Books

Adventure Stories for GIRLS and BOYS ...

TIMBER TRAIL RIDERS
The Long Trail North
The Texas Tenderfoot
The Luck of Black Diamond
Mystery of the Hollywood Horse
The Mysterious Dude

POWER BOYS SERIES
The Haunted Skyscraper
The Flying Skeleton

DONNA PARKER
In Hollywood
At Cherrydale
Special Agent
On Her Own
A Spring to Remember
Mystery at Arawak
Takes a Giant Step

TROY NESBIT SERIES
Sand Dune Pony
Diamond Cave Mystery
Indian Mummy Mystery
Mystery at Rustlers' Fort

New Stories About Your Television Favorites ...

Dr. Kildare
    Assigned to Trouble
    The Magic Key

Janet Lennon at Camp Calamity

Walt Disney's Annette
    Mystery at Smugglers' Cove
    Desert Inn Mystery
    Sierra Summer
    Mystery at Moonstone Bay
    Mystery at Medicine Wheel

Combat! The Counterattack

The Beverly Hillbillies

Lassie
    Secret of the Summer
    Forbidden Valley
    Mystery at Blackberry Bog

Lucy and the Madcap Mystery

Patty Duke and Mystery Mansion

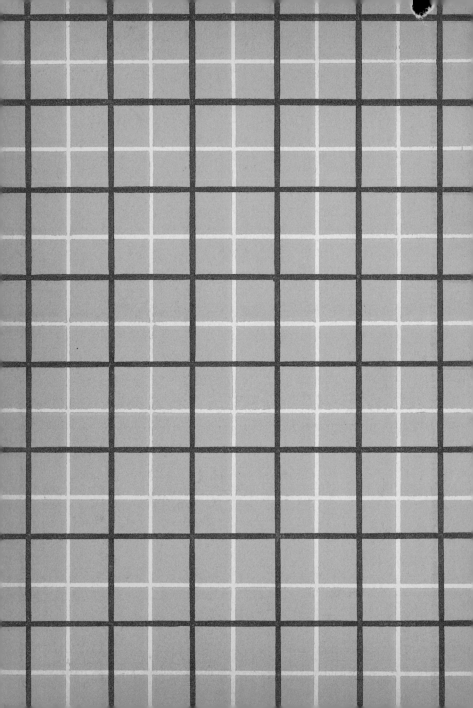